TAKING IT TO HEART

MARIE DESPLECHIN

TRANSLATED FROM THE FRENCH
BY WILL HOBSON

Granta Books
London

Granta Publications, 2/3 Hanover Yard, London N1 8BE

First published in Great Britain by Granta Books 2001
First published in French by Editions de l'Olivier/Le Seuil 1995

1 3 5 7 9 10 8 6 4 2

Typeset by M Rules
Printed and bound in Great Britain
by Mackays of Chatham PLC

CONTENTS

1

AN IMPORTANT QUESTION

HE WAS sitting on the sofa and I was grovelling at his feet. He was tanned, smooth-skinned and ravishing after a fortnight in Italy. I, on the other hand, was grey, haggard and over-wrought from working flat out every God-given day. I had hurried to let him in before the doorbell woke my children up. What a beautiful face, I'd thought as I opened the door. But it wasn't a thought which gave me pleasure just then. I was too tired. Instead I fixed him with a carcinogenic look.

He came into my flat with the beatific expression and med-itative gaze that on the train to Lourdes distinguishes the nuns from the boy scouts and the bedridden. The shy smile of the young bride before she trips up on the church carpet. The masterful stance of the teenager, alone in front of the mirror, carefully squeezing his first blackhead.

'I've just landed,' he murmured dreamily. As if a heli-copter had just dropped him on the roof.

'Oh! What time did the plane get in?' I couldn't seem to stop myself shouting hysterically.

1

'Nine, on the dot,' he breathed.

He tossed his jacket on to the sofa, where it landed like a feather. What grace, honestly, what grace he bestowed on everything he touched! Staggering. How do people manage to look so neat and carefully pressed the whole time? Do they keep elves under the floorboards of their flats who polish their shoes and iron their shirts every night?

I smoked nervously. I was dragging on my butt like a navvy, and I kept running my hand through my lank hair.

'Weren't you meant to be coming back tomorrow?' Now I was really bellowing. I seemed to have lost control of my nerves.

'Yes,' he said quietly. 'I changed my plans. I suddenly had enough of Italy and travelling and being on my own. I wanted to come back to Paris as quickly as possible. I left the beach, went straight to the airport and took the first plane I could.'

The Beach. The Airport. The Plane. What a hard life.

It was a good thing he'd thought to call from the airport.

'I'm at Orly,' he'd announced.

'Already?' I'd replied, horrified.

'Yes, I'm waiting for my bags. When I've picked them up, I'll get a taxi to my place, drop my stuff off, then I'll be round.'

'You'll be round?'

'Yes. See you in a sec.'

He had spoken very naturally – as if he had a guaranteed place in my home, as if my life included him in its daily routine. And then he'd hung up, and dashed off to get his luggage, leaving me no chance to gather my wits and suggest a different day, a more opportune moment. I

2

contemplated the silent telephone for a moment, dumb-founded. Then I looked up at Marc, who was gazing at me in disbelief, realizing that he was about to be shown the door. When we had only just managed to put the children to bed. When he was finally ready to read my palm. He'd arrived at my flat earlier in the evening, and I'd been comforted by his unexpected presence, like a breath of spring. But now Marc wasn't happy. No, he wasn't. He'd even gone white, which actually complemented his jet-black hair and red shirt beautifully. He was positively Garibaldian. And furious, too.

He paced up and down my three metres of carpet in silence, smoking and seething. I sat with my elbows on the cluttered table, my head bowed in contrition, equally speechless.

'So, do you love him?' he asked eventually, as if it was a question of love rather than an organizational cock-up.

'Oh, I don't know,' I said to the tablecloth, not daring to look at that handsome, betrayed face. 'Maybe.'

'What about me then? What about me?'

How could I answer him? I ventured, 'My husband always said I was a bigamist.'

It was hardly a proper answer. At best, it was tricksy. But he smiled.

'Fine, so you're a bigamist. But why kick me out so you can let him in?'

There it was. He had put his finger on it. Why one rather than the other? And above all – why the other and not him?

There was no way I could tell him. I didn't want to lose him, not yet; he was so sweet-natured and we were so close. I never wanted to give up the bird in the hand again. I didn't want to feel abandoned again, or experience the nights that drag on interminably, the silent telephone. Given the choice between Love and having people around, a thousand times people and never again Love. But try and explain that to someone you're about to throw out for the night. Try telling him that life has taught you to bargain with each of your feelings, one by one. That your heart is divided into compartments like a haberdasher's stall. That that's the price of your obligingness. Try telling him that and then duck to avoid the slap.

'It's just that there's an order,' I lied.

'What – oldest first?'

'No, I mean the order I got to know you in. Husband first, lover second.'

'That's all?'

'Yes, that's all.'

I hunched over and gave him a shifty look. I felt like a hypocrite. 'You shouldn't feel threatened. You know how much I love you, don't you?'

There, I'd said it. Maybe it was true, maybe it wasn't – who knows what loving involves? Who knows? Maybe I did really love him – this man who was now laughing quietly at my downcast expression. It was lucky he was fond of me. He could have hit me. Some women get their heads boiled for less. You read about it all the time in the papers.

He picked up his jacket. I stood up and walked him to the door, my heart torn with shame and regret.

'Call me tomorrow,' he said finally as he left, a trace of resentment in the lines round his eyes. 'And tell me about it.'

I admit it was nothing to be proud of. But it was dealt with. Tomorrow, tomorrow life would be sweeter.

Tomorrow I would love better. Tomorrow I would be able to earn forgiveness for all the wrongs I'd done and even for those still to come. Tomorrow. But first there was this Soon which now consumed me entirely.

For the moment I had nothing to do but wait, drowning in the thousands of seconds that separate a promise from its fulfilment. A lot of the questions people ask about time are far too abstract. I'll tell you what time is all about. In so far as it affects the lives of humans, it's easily quantified. It can be measured by the number of things a woman can do to fix up her ravaged flat while a taxi is speeding from Orly South to Paris at night.

That is to say, I cleared the table and broke all the glasses in the process.

And then there he was, the prodigal, smelling of holidays. He solemnly took in everything in my untidy flat, as if he was giving it his blessing.

'Are you well?' I said loudly, startling him, as he walked through the door.

'I'm fine.' He looked deep into my eyes as if he had just dropped a ten-franc coin into them.

'I'll make some tea,' I exclaimed, making a sharp turn. 'I hope I don't scald myself,' I continued from the far end of the kitchen, chattering away like a runaway train, 'It wouldn't be very clever ending up in casualty, especially now the children are asleep.'

I was losing it. The kitchen looked like a bombed-out city. There were coffee grounds all over the sink. It took a while to find the spattered teapot amid the debris. As the water boiled, I started cleaning up, muttering to myself as I did so. It was so quiet I thought he must have started meditating. Fine: as long as he didn't bang into the ceiling if he managed to levitate. But no, he was choosing a record. Liszt. He'd chosen Liszt. This man who liked nothing better than waking up late on a Sunday morning and taking a long shower, the sun streaming through the windows on to the polished floorboards, to the accompaniment of the likes of Biggie Smalls. Liszt. *La lugubre gondola*? *La Marche funèbre*? Or *Sunt Lacrimae Rerum*?

Sunt Lacrimae Rerum. At full volume. The piano whined to me personally. I felt as though I was going to start crying. But I didn't. Instead I almost scalded myself and set the dishcloth on fire.

To be honest, I was wondering what he had to tell me that was so urgent he'd had to rush over the minute he'd dropped from the sky. I'd never known him to be in such a hurry. Quite the opposite. He was more the parsimonious sort – fickle, treacherous, always spreading himself thinly, never staying more than two nights in a row. And as unfriendly on the second night as a man delivering ice cream to the back of beyond in the middle of July. But what grace, the first night – what talent!

Oh, this bloody three-nights business! People read too much fiction . . . It's been a decade now since the amorous bragging peddled in books like *The Unbearable Lightness of Being* first incited legions of lovers to deny tired young women the comfort of their arms on the third night. This ubiquitous erotic manual means that nights have become like so many pots of yoghurt. Seduction – consumption – expiry. It's not a novel concept – it's been hanging around bars and garrison towns for thousands of years. But freshly decked out and amiably propounded by a man with an urbane turn of phrase, this three-nights business has become the scourge of the age. Oh, the power of rhetoric. These are melancholy times.

Anyway. Third night or no third night, what's the difference to a woman who has surrendered on the first? None. So what if the novel reader disappears the morning after the second night with all the predictability and blithe unconcern of a metronome? When he decides to return, two, four or six nights later, she's still going to open her arms to him. This is how it's been since time began, and it was the same for me. For four years, I'd been passionately granting first nights, then immolating third nights on the altar of literature, sacrifices to Baal Moloch ritualized as a game of musical chairs. Given all this, who would bother to invoke the glorious name of love? And yet . . .

After I'd spilled half the contents of the teapot on the grimy carpet, he said: 'I've got something to tell you.'

'Ah ha!' I shouted. 'As I suspected.'

Still, I was shocked. Prepare yourself, my girl. Compose your thoughts; not everything in life is good to hear. First deal with that colossal depressive whose keening is still filling the flat. Kill Liszt, fast. I leaped on the stereo.

'This guy's creepy,' I blurted out. 'I think I'll shut him up.'

I strangled Liszt. *Gluk*, went the piano. I changed the record, jabbed *Play* fiercely and straight away a gang of renegade black guys set up a wailing that sounded like the cries of a lone psychopath. The familiar racket drew a soothing veil over my agitation. I ran over to the fireplace and began rummaging in the soot.

'Wait, I'll make a fire.'

I stacked the last of the branches from the Christmas tree in the blackened hearth in a frenzy. Needles scattered all over the carpet, working their way pitilessly into the tiny gaps between the thousands of crumbs already in residence. On top of the pyre I put two of those dry bricks which are only found in Parisian grocers'. I swear, that weirdly compacted wood has never been a part of a moist, living tree. They must be mass-produced by slaves chained up in cellars. They burn with an aggressive sniggering sound. Before I'd even put the match to the wood, the flames leaped up. The smoke from the inferno instantly made black streaks on the marble mantelpiece. My face burned, my cheeks flushed and my eyes felt feverish.

'Ah,' I said, looking over at him with idiotic pride, 'now that really is nice.'

He was sitting on the carpet, legs nonchalantly stretched out in front of him, his face raised to the ceiling, meditative.

'OK, that's enough. Come and sit down,' he requested smoothly, with a hint of a smile.

No heavy, lecherous look, no pitiful, plaintive expression, just a sort of manly self-assurance. What was the matter with him?

'Are you well . . . Really well?' I insisted.

'Yes. Yes, yes.'

Not ill. No money worries. No family problems. So?

'I did a lot of thinking in Italy,' he began.

'Oh no,' I thought.

I sank down into the sofa. I was wondering where I'd find enough indulgence in me to be receptive to an account of the Great Return from Italy when behind me, in the passage, a faint scratching suddenly drowned out the tumult of the surrounding world.

8

'Mum,' a small voice said, 'Mum, I've had a nightmare.'

I turned round and opened my tireless arms. Automatic gestures like this – perfectly suited responses – seem to have been passed down from a primitive age, intuited from an ancestral store of feelings.

'Come here, sweetheart,' I said naturally, not needing to think about my words at all, 'my angel.'

My tall, pale-lipped daughter came and stood in front of me, pretending not to see the smiling man sitting on the carpet. She took her designated place in the crook of my thighs and pressed her pointed nose into the shelter of my neck. I buried all my thought and all my cares in her thin, curly hair. If she'd found her place, my frail little monkey, you could say I'd found mine too.

'I don't want to go to sleep any more, I want to stay with you,' she said.

'Don't worry. You are with me.'

My daughter told me her nightmare. It was full of deaths and kidnappings, fear and separation. When she eventually said, 'and then I woke up,' I could feel the nightmare wriggling inside me like a fish in a net. She'd talked and now it was my turn to feel the terrors of separation and estrangement. She, on the other hand, was smiling, her frown gone, her fluttering eyelashes chasing away the last remnants of the dream. And what did it matter if the backwash of a mother's fears was swilling around in me, because I was old and she was as fresh as a new shoot. We are just the grumbling mechanisms children drag behind them as they run along the paths of time.

'Well, now,' I said, 'it's only a nightmare. We'll sort it out. Because nightmares are fierce, tricky little creatures, but they have one sworn enemy: milk.'

'Milk?' my daughter asked with that joyous incredulity which makes us love them.

'Hot milk shrivels up nightmares and squashes them flat. So now both of us are going to go to the kitchen to heat up some milk and when it's cooled down you're going to drink it. After that, you'll see, the nightmare will disappear and sleep will come flying back on its soft wings.'

'On its soft wings, do you think so?'

I stood up and sat my daughter on my hip. She sucked her thumb, her feet dangling against my calves. Hips are a good place to carry children as long as they're not twenty centimetres taller than you.

As we passed in front of my visitor, who was now distractedly flicking through my records, probably wanting to put a stop to the cries of the ghetto, I realized that I had forgotten about him; he'd left the real world at the exact moment my daughter entered it. Because now I saw only what my daughter saw. We were a single pair of eyes, a single indifferent being picking its way gracefully through the human disarray of the evening.

In the kitchen the mess now seemed like nothing more terrible than the comforting muddle of everyday life. We watched the milk come to the boil in the saucepan. My daughter's slender body stayed glued to mine, two upright bodies, one still not touching the ground.

When she'd drained her bowl to the last drop, we went and sat back down in front of the fireplace. The fire was crackling furiously. I flashed an apologetic smile at the man who sat cross-legged beside the fire, leafing through an old paper. He responded with a discreet nod. I was grateful to him for not interrupting the affectionate course of events with loud words.

But my daughter intercepted the exchange. She darted a nosy glance at our guest who simply smiled calmly, half-bent over his paper.

'I think it's time to go back to bed now,' I said to the little sharp-eyed person. 'It's late, it's the middle of the night.'

'What about you?' asked my daughter. 'Are you going to bed?'

'Yes, in a while.'

'Soon?'

'Yes, soon. Probably.'

'OK.'

She got up, and twirled round between us, showing off her slender, precious self to our twin gaze. She was wearing a threadbare, sleeveless cotton nightie.

'I'm The Nearly Naked Girl,' she said, lowering her chin to admire herself.

'Well, come on then, Miss Nearly Naked, I'm putting you to bed.'

She let herself be picked up in my strong arms, wrapping her legs round my waist.

In their bedroom her brother was fast asleep, his head buried in the pillow, his hands either side of his handsome face. I put her in her bed, next to his, and kissed her on the cheek.

'Another kiss, Mum,' she said when I straightened up.

I complied without quibbling, then headed for the door.

'Night, night, sweetheart,' I said in a low voice.

'Night, night, little bunny,' she sang out, cheeky and content.

'There we are,' I said as I came back into the living room. I sat back down and looked at him with the same expression as before, as if nothing had happened. But in my brief absence the world had shifted. Everything was different. Imperceptibly but irrefutably different. I was no longer in exactly the same place I had been. I had stopped spinning like a dervish in the whirling present. Walking through the children's room had anchored me with a past and a future that now formed two comfortable lead insoles in my shoes.

'Is everything alright?' he asked kindly, showing that it was sensitivity rather than a lack of interest which had made him keep his distance while I'd been looking after my daughter.

'Yes, it's fine. She should go back to sleep now.'

I sighed tenderly.

'So, what was it you had to tell me that was so important?'

Life's a funny game of cards, isn't it? You only have to pay a little attention to the hand in progress to realize that the deal is constantly changing. As if the cards are slyly dealing themselves. I, who a quarter of an hour earlier had been doing a convincing impression of a madwoman, was now the soul of serenity. Whereas the man who had previously seemed so majestic was now fidgeting on the carpet like a timid little rabbit.

'Oh,' he said, trying to look nonchalant. 'Nothing really.'

'Come on,' I insisted, 'something must have happened to make you rush back to Paris in such a hurry.'

'Yeah. Sure.'

'Wasn't it nice? Wasn't the weather good?'

No need to worry on that score. The weather had been good, wonderful, even. Italy still had its black volcanoes, its pink houses turned in on the shade, and the ancient sea still

12

bathed it, murmuring promises. He had sped along neglected roads and lingered in flower-covered hotels. He had strolled down streets not yet overrun by Franco-German hordes, rubbing shoulders with hurrying Italian men and ravishing Italian women. He had read behind drawn blinds and gone swimming off white beaches.

'Lovely,' I interjected every now and again, rubbing my hands to show I was paying attention and to encourage him to continue. 'But come on,' I said eventually, 'what happened? Weren't you glad to be there?'

'Yes I was, very glad. Until yesterday. Yesterday I had supper on the terrace of my hotel. You know I'm not afraid of being alone, the opposite really. I looked at the sea, I felt happy. Some children were playing, running about between the tables. A few people were having supper. When it started to get late, I folded up my newspaper and went up to my room. I read some more and then I fell asleep on my book.

'And then in the middle of the night I woke up, covered in sweat. I never usually remember my dreams, but I'd just had a sort of nightmare which completely terrified me. I was driving along a road, trying to escape, frantically looking for somewhere to hide. But pretty soon I realized that there was nowhere I could go. It was pitch dark and I was alone.

'I was being chased. I tried to see the face of my pursuer. At least if I can find out who it is, I thought, I'll be less afraid. This is what I was thinking as I sat behind the steering wheel when suddenly I saw, clearly, what was threatening me in the darkness. Death was chasing me, death itself, the one you dread as a child, the one that takes the living away from the world forever. Instead of subsiding, my fear became unbearable. I woke up.

'I tried to go back to sleep. But the feeling was still there; it got stronger and stronger. I tossed and turned on my bed for ages. Then I got up, dressed and packed my bag. I went down to reception and settled my bill with an ancient porter who was half-asleep. I left and drove for hours. I didn't have a clue where to go. I said to myself that I was going to drive north, towards France.

'But the further I went, the less reassured I felt. Time had started to move very slowly. It felt as if the night would never end. The nightmare was carrying on, and it felt exactly the same, now I was awake, as it had when I was asleep. I couldn't stop thinking about death chasing me.

'When it began to get light, I stopped at the first café I found open. I drank a very strong espresso and tried to think how I was going to get out of this nightmare. That was when I thought of you, of your flat with all its things, of your children.

'OK, I said to myself, I'll go and see her and tell her what's happening. She's bound to be at home because of the children. If she's not, I'll hang around outside and wait until she comes back. She'll make me a cup of tea, I'll tell her what's happened and she'll listen. Without knowing very clearly why, this plan completely calmed me down. Right, I thought, I'm going to go to her place, as if the idea of dashing from the south of Italy to the eleventh arrondissement in Paris was the most reasonable one I'd ever had. I'll tell her my little story and everything will be better.

'Feeling calmer, I left the café. I got behind the steering wheel again. The sun rose up over the sea. I looked at the map and decided to catch a plane in Naples. Eleventh arrondissement, I said to myself as I drove along. Eleventh arrondissement, Driver, and make it snappy, please.'

'Didn't you like Italy any more?' I asked, confused. I wasn't prepared for finding myself catapulted to the heart of his man's story.

'No, I adored Italy. I looked at it like a lover, its white stones and its fig trees. But the fact that I knew I was leaving made me all the happier to be there. I left my car at the airport and ran and bought a ticket for the first flight to Paris. As I waited for it to leave, I studied the sky for a long time. And I told myself that I had to ask you an important question.'

While he talked, I felt my eyelids drooping. I listened, half-dozing, my head resting on the arm of the sofa, a bleary smile on my lips, involuntarily daydreaming of my grandmother – her blue eyes, her little house with the painted walls, the woodpigeons cooing in the mornings. It wasn't that I was bored, but it was very late and I felt peaceful, and being at peace makes me go to sleep. The murmur of his voice lulled me on my ocean of memory. His words seemed to reach me from far away, the end of the world, the mainland's last landing stage.

'Lift up your head so I can see your eyes.'

To be honest, it was the silence that followed this request that roused me from my blissful languor. Oh no, I had to return. I had to quit the halfway houses of time, leave behind my amiable drowsiness, the hazy border of dreams and thought. It was time to return to rational meaning what belongs to music. So soon.

I stared wide-eyed. In my sleepy state, I hadn't noticed him come over to me. His face was now very close to mine. With a sense of miraculous gratitude, I rediscovered the familiar features, the deep, brown eyes, the straight nose and, best of all, the mouth, its lips like walled gardens, embroideries, fountains. So, I hadn't left the field of dreams. This man leaning over me was the entire known world, the childhood and death of things, the tumult of storms and the still of the artist's studio.

I looked deep into his eyes. I could read clearly what lay in their watchful gaze. He'd come back to ask me to share his life. And now he was waiting. He hoped I'd be surprised, as if I didn't already know, and hadn't known forever, what he was going to say to me.

'I wanted,' he said, 'to ask you to come and live with me.'

There, the time had come. Fortune had eaten its tail and we had entered the loop of our story. I tried to feign shock. I raised my eyebrows. My mouth opened slightly. But, deep down, I was purring, I was the great snake of time.

'God,' I said. 'With my children?'

'Yes, with your children. Well?'

Well, I didn't even need to think. I woke up. I returned violently to the world.

'Uh, no,' I said. 'It's no.'

'No?'

His eyes bolted out of his head. I disappeared into the sofa. I felt broken, like grain pounded for a long time in a mortar. Like a body turned to flour. Who proposes marriage to a bag of flour?

'Look,' I said. 'I've been at work all day. I've got enough to worry about as it is, what with money, work, the children. Not to mention secondary matters such as trying to maintain some kind of personal life and keeping this place clean. My heart is like a burnt-up desert. I spend the whole time shoring up my life and just hearing the word "tomorrow" makes me want to cry. What do you expect me to say?'

'Well, Yes, of course. All you've got to do is say Yes, that takes care of your heart and the business of where to live. As for work and the children, I can't say. But who knows? Why not?'

'Oh,' I groaned, 'I don't know where I've put my brain. Maybe another time, another day, when I've got used to the idea. You can stay if you like, we can go to bed, but please don't ask me anything else.'

He left the same night – bewildered in turn and suddenly reserved. I shut the door behind him, overcome by a strange exhaustion. I went to bed alone, my throat thick, feeling pummelled like a fairground boxer. I slept.

I was working the next day so I got up early. I took my skipping children to school.

'Do you remember my nightmare?' my daughter asked me on the way, her hand in my left hand, her schoolbag on my back.

'Yes, poppet. It didn't come back, did it?'

'No,' she said, after considering the question for a moment.

'I knew it wouldn't. Because that's what we are. We are the nightmare tamers. We are the masters of dreams.'

'Really?' my son said, hanging off my right arm, his face creased with early morning tiredness.

'Yes, really,' I assured him proudly, as if words could make the world.

'Cool,' said my son, shrugging his shoulders to adjust his overloaded schoolbag.

Standing in front of the school, I watched them dart through the bottle-green gates. I desperately wanted to keep them close to my beating heart, to give them sun in winter and happiness in all weathers. It wasn't possible, of course. We had to go our separate ways.

17

I was deep in thought all day, good for nothing, vacant and locked away in the towers of my mind.

When evening came I was still pondering. After I'd put the children to bed, I sat on the sofa next to the telephone, thinking. The phone barely had time to ring before I picked it up.

'You bastard,' said Marc. 'You said you'd ring me.'

'I was going to,' I said. 'I swear, I was just about to ring you.'

'I don't know if I should believe you. Anyway, I don't.'

'Why not?'

'Because whenever you're caught blatantly lying or being ungrateful, you always manage to turn things to your advantage and put the other person in the wrong. So don't tell me you were going to ring me when the fact is that you didn't call me.'

'But I swear, Marc . . .'

'Don't swear, whatever you do, don't *swear*! It's so infuriating – your obsession with justifying yourself.'

'God, you're so annoying! What's the point of calling if all you want to do is make a scene in the middle of the night? Why don't you try later when you've managed to calm down?'

'Alright,' said Marc, 'don't get angry. The way you fly off the handle amazes me. So, how was your day?'

'Fine,' I said. 'How about yours?'

We were off, describing the day's events in minute detail, dipping into its basket of minor irritations and slight surprises, thoroughly immersed in the mundane and temporarily oblivious to the bigger picture.

'By the way,' Marc said, suddenly, 'how did yesterday evening turn out?'

'Fine,' I answered, shamefacedly. 'About that. There's something you should know. I'm probably going to move in with him.'

'What? With him? He asked you to live with him?'

'Yes.'

'And you said yes, of course! And you're happy about that, are you?'

'Yes. I think so. I've thought about it a lot and now I'm sure. I'm happy.'

'That,' said Marc, after a moment of heavy silence, 'that really is the limit.'

2

At Sea

It was an adorable little boat, bobbing coquettishly among a hundred similar-sized craft in a marina on the Mediterranean, not far from Cannes. I walked across the gangway. I went aboard. It was the wrong thing to do. If I couldn't exercise common sense, I could at least have used my memory. Didn't I retain, seared into my synapses, every catatonia-inducing detail of an interminable sea voyage I had taken part in a few years earlier, off La Rochelle?

On that occasion I'd gone on board with my husband and a couple of his friends at the end of October, a time of year when – according to certain corrupt Druids on the regional council – there's still a little sun left in the Vendée skies. God. The cold, the rain, the wind! Calamities which I am *capable* of enduring – but only when I'm at home on the carpet by my fireplace, close to my tobacconist and my newsagent; then I'm even contemptuous. 'Go on then!' I shout sarcastically at the elements. 'Do your worst! Vent your spleen!'

But on a boat one's relationship with the elements is obviously a little different. Because suddenly you're the one they're venting their spleen on. The elements are just like the rest of us: if you give them a chance to harm you personally, they'll take it. In fact, they'll push it. So let's not talk about the fact that the boat had barely left port before I was soaked, frozen, *lacerated* by the whistling, damp, salty wind. Honestly, the sea: what a disaster.

And perhaps we shouldn't mention, either, the extreme irritation aroused in me by my companions in disaster. Irritation which, unfortunately, I couldn't blame on the boat. It's not as if we'd ever had much in common even on land, even in Paris, in the seventh arrondissement. They were conventional – boring. Let's call them Navy Blue and Bottle Green.

'Everything up to scratch, darling?' yelled Navy Blue. She was dressed as Skipper Barbie in boots and oilskins and hanging from a stubbornly taut rope in the seaspray. In fact, *swinging* on it like a thing possessed, with the kind of love and vigour which in other circumstances she might have devoted to the performance of an extremely specialized sex act.

'Bloody hell, make fast that rope, won't you!' roared Bottle Green, standing with his legs splayed and teeth clenched and holding the tiller virilely steady in the storm.

Normally they were an ordinary little couple, pretty unremarkable, really. But on that boat, with her hanging like a sole in the ropes and him glued to his tiller, they suddenly took on an entirely different dimension. A celestial, splendidly pornographic dimension. Venus Anadyomene and Captain Ahab. I would have killed myself laughing if I hadn't already been dying, face-down in the water sloshing around Captain Ahab's feet, my stomach churning.

As for my husband – who adored the sea (and who was in turn adored by my mother, but that's another story) – he was shimmying like plankton from one end of the bridge to the other. Wriggling, multiform, ungraspable. He screwed and unscrewed, made fast and made loose, pulled and released everything he could get his hands on, buffeted by a gale of threats and counter-orders. And he did it all as if this pathetic bustling about on a cockleshell was the sole purpose of his existence.

He would have done better to look after me. It was my first boat trip. And I was busily applying the remnants of my consciousness to swearing that it was going to be my last, if I survived that long. Curled up in a ball on the lumpy plastic decking of the cockpit, my teeth chattering, I visualized turning my body inside out like a glove. I visualized gutting it like a freshly caught fish. I visualized evisceration and shipwreck. If only I could make it stop! Once and for all!

'Don't you want to go below?' a sodden voice cried in my ear.

'I'd rather throw myself overboard.'

Those were my last conscious words.

I didn't open my mouth again for the rest of the two-day trip. At the time things were already delicate between me and my husband. And that maritime nightmare joined the sad list of marital resentments under the heading Betrayal and Abandonment of a Person in Danger.

'Never again,' I remember repeating to myself, back on dry land but feeling so ill and wretched that I had to lie down on the cobblestones of the marina, indifferent to the disgusted looks of the passers-by.

But everyone knows about Never Again. Swearing oaths, experience – nothing makes us any better at it. We remain the gullible victims of our curiosity, weakness and opportunism. And that goes for boats as well as everything else.

'It's June, not November,' my adorable boyfriend remarked, with shining eyes and a smile like a Cheshire cat.

He was driving, and every now and then we pushed back our sunglasses to squint at the palm trees flashing by along the promenade. The sunshine drummed on the car. My toes kept time nonchalantly to the cheerful strains of Stevie Wonder.

'The other thing you have to remember is that this is Cannes, not Brest,' he continued, when we were walking arm in arm in the shade of the umbrella pines. 'Look!' he said, gesturing to the distant purples, unfurling the whole horizon with a sweep of his arm. 'Look how calm the sea is! My father would love to spend the day with us. Ask your son if he wants to bring a friend. We'll take care of everything. Once you're on board you won't have to do a thing except float along and fall asleep with the sun on your face.'

The crickets chirped, the air was balmy and sweet, the light and shade was picking out the faintest nuances of light and shade: in short, as per usual, the Mediterranean South was one giant aphrodisiac cliché.

'Are you sure I won't feel sick?' I said, wrinkling my nose.

'Why are you always pulling faces?' He stared at me curiously. As if I make faces by choice rather than through necessity, compelled as I am to express those thousands of little emotions which come too quickly and constantly to put into words.

'What's to stop us from going on Léon's boat?' my son asked in turn, that evening, taking a rare break from his belligerent internal monologue. 'Are you scared?'

'No, I'm not scared.'

'So let's go, then,' he said. 'And stop pulling faces all the time. It doesn't look nice.'

A string of Chinese lanterns bathed the terrace in soft light. The evening was warm and alive.

'I'm only saying that because I like you,' he added.

The three of us were having breakfast when, over the top of my coffee cup, I said, 'OK. OK. When do we go aboard?'

'Go aboard?' repeated my boyfriend, feigning surprise.

'Go aboard your father's boat, stupid!'

'Oh, right. Are you going to come, then?'

He smiled at me and my ice-cream heart instantly melted in my chest, flooding me with vanilla waves.

'Cool,' said my son.

'Sweetheart, it'll all be perfect, I promise,' my boyfriend said.

I had no illusions, but nonetheless I agreed with an alacrity that surprised me. Because one thing seemed certain – if perfection existed at all, it was here, in his morning smile, in my son's happiness, in the light bathing the sea front. At that moment I couldn't have cared less about what was going to happen next. People say: A bird in the hand is worth two in the bush. But I'd be more specific: If you're in love at breakfast, who cares about supper?

Léon was waiting for us on the quay. We could see his diminutive silhouette bustling around the ropes from some way off. My son scampered ahead, dragging along the friend we'd just torn from the bosom of his family. Running along one behind the other and calling out loudly to Léon, the two little boys seemed to trace a fine line of light through time.

All along the quay, tethered boats were bobbing up and down like well-behaved dogs, nodding their muzzles and wagging their tails energetically. If it hadn't been for the frenetic bustle of the weekend sailors jumping around like ticks on the neighbouring decks, the quay would have looked the very picture of calm contentment. I hesitated to take my boyfriend's hand: I was afraid of looking ridiculous, conscious of our age. When we reached the boat, the boys and I kissed Léon.

We left port in the singing morning. The fishermen on the jetty were still within view when I felt my heart cut gently loose from its arteries and sink like a weight to the pit of my stomach, even though I was sitting comfortably beside the tiller. It wasn't exactly chilly, but it wasn't exactly warm, either. The sun was just strumming on the tips of the tiny waves. I tried to listen to Léon's account of his trips up and down the Riviera.

As nature abhors a vacuum, so Léon abhorred the sedentary life. It was an all-encompassing abhorrence, although never expressed as such, which left him exhausted, grouchy and aggrieved after three winter months spent at home in Paris. The minute a couple of artless and unconvincing little suns appeared on the TV weather map, he'd take out his suitcase, throw in his flip-flops and life jacket and start mumbling to his resigned family about going away. More often than not, three days after that he'd be gone.

He liked to travel, meandering from west to east in his big car. Having said that, he'd always reach his destination – the

South – and the port where his boat was waiting in no time at all. Then he'd hoist the sails and life would begin again, full of hurried departures, temporary arrivals and messages on the answering machine.

So there we were, Léon chatting away while I tried to listen, when all at once the top came and sat on the bottom; the bottom rebelled; and suddenly I had an overwhelming desire to faint. Well done me. I'd asked for it and now it had happened. I was ill. I cast a resentful look at the sea. It looked innocuous, perfectly smooth, its pretty little waves sparkling in a gentle breeze. The sea – that vile, hypocritical *stuff*.

'Are you ill?' asked Léon, who was thoughtful and considerate, giving me a worried look.

'I'm not sure,' I answered feebly. 'I think I feel sick.'

I stared fixedly ahead of me, trying to avoid the nauseating shimmering of the waves. Don't move, whatever you do, don't move and maybe everything will return to its proper place. I was sitting there, stiff and motionless, when out of the corner of my eye I suddenly caught sight of my son and his friend leaning over the side-rail. No doubt they were going to lose their balance and topple overboard and be swallowed up in our pitiless wake. Terrible. But I couldn't lift a finger. Nausea had harnessed me to the crushing yoke of Resignation. Possessed by Fate, as unresisting as a Calvinist, I watched them hurtling towards their destiny without batting an eyelid.

They didn't fall in. Thank God. But I heard a dismayed exclamation ring out clearly in the sea air, 'Oh no, my glasses!'

'Panic stations,' I murmured. '*Five-hundred franc* glasses.'

In the process of leaning over, the little klutz had lost the prescription sunglasses which his father had given him strict orders to wear when we left. He looked up, distraught, and his myopic gaze slowly swept the horizon. I had the impression he was looking for me.

'That wasn't very clever,' I shouted from my seat of pain. 'What am I going to tell your father?' Temporarily restored to a more contemporary view of destiny, I added, 'And stop leaning over like that! You'll end up falling in!'

'But we're fishing!' my son retorted cheekily.

I didn't have the strength to react. I left it to Léon to restore order on board and gave myself wholly over to nausea.

Actually I would have preferred not to dwell too deeply on what was happening inside me. A strong instinct, probably hailing from that distant time when all of us humans were fish, told me that the best thing to do in such circumstances was to think about something else. As if an average westerner – without any training in meditation – has a hope of distracting herself from her seasickness by mere force of will. Fat chance.

I decided to concentrate on the first idea, or shred of an idea my neurons fired at me – the infinite diversity of animal life. So I thought about fishes, the millions of members of their species going about their businesses at that very moment, down below, deep in that homogeneous, dense and threatening whole that we call the sea. I thought about them intensely, about those fundamentally alien things that thrive and rot in the water, about those active, slimy . . . and, anyway, there I concluded my efforts at concentration. I stared at my hands. They were covered in a thin film of sweat. Ideas were no use to me. Better to empty my mind, hide away in nothingness, take refuge in the

Great Merciful Blank. Closedown, the peace of the test card, indifference.

I stared blurrily at the red plastic bowl on the seat opposite me. Tied to this landmark, my mental state fell into step with the insistent rhythm of our progress. *Splash, splash,* went my stomach, banging against the fragile wall of my diaphragm. I swallowed painfully. I felt myself decomposing and wondered if I was taking the first step towards emptiness.

I didn't have the chance to take the experiment further because, like a racing car careering off a track, the emaciated figure of St Francis Xavier crashed into my empty mind. St Francis Xavier, budding Jesuit and missionary to Japan. St Francis Xavier, bound for Asia from Lisbon, tossed about like a straw down the coast of Africa. St Francis Xavier, suffering from unremitting seasickness and for some reason convinced that the way to overcome nausea was to eat fish entrails. St Francis Xavier, who, after all that, died on board – no one even knows what of – and was dumped like a bin liner on an island in the China Sea. A man who managed to escape the Inquisitors and the Japanese, killed by a mere voyage and hurriedly buried on heathen soil. The sea: what a disaster, what a complete disaster!

Eat fish entrails. Eat fish entrails. Eat fish entrails.

'Léon,' I said weakly, 'I don't feel well.'

'Why don't you go and lie down,' Léon said. 'It'll pass, you'll see.'

In the meantime my boyfriend had become very active in a way that suggested a convincing familiarity with boats, their joys and constraints. After inspecting the cabin of his father's old tub with the meticulousness of a private detective (Oh, did you break the compass? Have you thought about rosé for lunch?), he had dressed, or rather undressed, for the occasion, leaving on nothing but a pair of tartan boxer shorts, a grey cotton T-shirt and some Docksiders. I contented myself with admiring his slim legs.

Before getting started on fiddling about with sails and ropes, he pissed virilely overboard. At once I bombarded my bladder with silent instructions to behave with the strictest continence. If there is one challenge that the lover of land and its comforts dreads above all others, it's got to be that of pissing overboard.

Anyway, he was running about, oblivious to the ridiculousness that inevitably arises from a combination of agitated behaviour and confined space, when his father called to him, 'Come and take the helm instead of me, I think your girlfriend's feeling ill.' He came over super quick.

'What's wrong?' he asked, as if he didn't know, putting his hand on my thigh in a brotherly way. 'Maybe you're too hot? Look at you, you're all wrapped up as if we're going through the Bering Straits. At least take off your polo neck!'

'No,' I said, hugging my chest sadly, 'I'm keeping my jumper on. I'm frozen.'

Unfortunately it was true. They were all prancing about half-naked and I was shivering. I didn't give a damn if I looked silly. I can't guarantee that I wouldn't have put a beanie on too, if there'd been one on board, for once forgetting my hatred of hats.

Let's not talk about those painful moments, let's not. I turned over in my seat, my face to the hull. I languished there, wretched, incapable even of proper resentment, just managing a vague sensation of hatred. I languished with such commitment that in the end I dozed off. Protected by sleep's feathered wings, time slipped by without me. Beside me the helmsman silently kept watch, flirtatiously offering his nose and shoulders to the tender sun. Sometimes the best moments are the ones you know nothing about. I slept innocently, a poor little thing wrapped up in summer, until my son's shouts woke me. From the other end of the boat he was yelling at the top of his voice, 'Mum! Mum! Look what we've caught!'

No doubt having decided that I'd slept enough, Léon and his son were letting him yell, not caring that I'd probably be woken up and therefore returned to my misery.

'Jellyfish,' my son said triumphantly, waving his bucket under my nose. In which, sure enough, quivering like some vile gelatine, was an array of jellyfish mingling their dubious-looking translucencies and feebly twitching their thin appendages in the cloudy water.

'Jellyfish, how horrible!' I said, dismayed.

'Yes, awful,' agreed my son. 'Aren't they beautiful, with all their colours?'

'Very beautiful,' I said, looking at him carefully.

Despite the sunlight, he looked deathly pale. I glanced at his short-sighted friend. He too had acquired an interesting pallor.

'Do you feel OK, boys?'

'Hmmm,' said my son, sitting down heavily beside me.

'Puh,' said his friend, hanging his head.

I looked around me. The waves now had a little white foam at their crests. The sails were bulging prettily. The wind had risen.

'I'm cold,' said my son.

'Me too,' agreed his friend.

Two minutes later they were lying in the cockpit, swathed in blankets which had been dug up from the cabin. The dashing little sailboat, which moments before had been a little ship setting cheerfully out from the port, bathed in sunlight, now resembled nothing so much as a floating hospital. My boyfriend gloomily studied the three useless bodies cluttering up his deck.

'Usually,' he said affably, 'people lying down on boats are wearing swimming costumes and sunbathing.'

'Yes, yes,' I replied bitterly, 'I'm sure you can come up with better memories of other boat trips.'

He raised his eyebrows. 'Oh, yes. That wouldn't be hard.'

Why do people have to have pasts? We should be able to put all that behind us, shouldn't we?

'Well, perhaps you should bring someone else next time.'

'Maybe I should. I'll think about it.'

'Good idea, do some thinking for a change.'

After all, if he was so keen on going sailing, all he had to do was call up one of those overgrown girl guides in galoshes, or one of those little bits of fluff in swimming costumes, who don't have hearts or livers or stomachs or imaginations. There was no point blaming me for being me, a person with a sensitive inner ear and a trail of vomiting children in tow. People have to know what they want in life. He was the one who had dragged me, protesting, on to this floating thing which makes you ill in the first place; and now, on top of everything else, I had to put up with his incessant reproaches. Oh, this was definitely the last time I was going on a boat. And it was also the last time I was going on holiday with a guy who dreamed about going sailing with another woman.

'Don't take it badly, please,' he said suddenly, jutting out his jaw. 'The children are sick, you're in a huff – the day's ruined – but it's not that bad, really. There'll be other days . . .'

'Not with me, sunshine,' I murmured inwardly, 'not with me, I promise.'

It's not just money worries that make people touchy; health worries do too. And neither of them is particularly character-building, I think that's self-evident. Except, perhaps, for St Francis Xavier.

We continued to rock on the spiteful waves. Above us ever-increasing numbers of slender clouds chased each other at high speed across the sky. The sails flapped and every now and then another boat raced past us.

'Léon!' called my soon-to-be-ex-boyfriend.

Léon poked his head out of the cabin stairs.

'Léon, what are you doing?'

'I'm making us something to eat,' said Léon, wiping his hands on a huge dishcloth. 'It's time, don't you think?'

'Are we going to land to have lunch?' I said weakly.

Léon smiled kindly. 'No, my dear, it's not the right place for it here. We're going to go towards the shore to find somewhere peaceful, then we'll drop anchor and have lunch on board. Is that OK with you?' he asked, giving his son a fraught look full of concern.

Lunch on board. All the fish entrails you can eat. Did they want to kill me with their reinforced concrete stomachs?

'I'm not hungry,' my son wailed to the wind.

'Pass me that bowl,' sighed his friend. 'I think I might be sick, if I can.'

'Perhaps lunch on board isn't such a good idea,' my

boyfriend observed eventually, without taking his eyes off the vague horizon.

'Really?' said Léon, rolling his dishcloth into a ball. 'Why not?' He looked disappointed.

'Take a look. You'll see.'

Léon contemplated the three prone bodies, then raised his eyes to the sky. His expression turned from disappointed to thoroughly dismayed.

'Don't they like the boat?' he asked his son, as if the latter was the only reliable intermediary between him and this confusing world.

'It's the boat that doesn't like us,' I said with a heroic smile.

Perfect: not content with having secretly decided to split up the minute I was back on solid ground, now I was disappointing Léon as he generously shared the thing he loved best with us. What a disastrous day, what a fiasco! And whose fault was it?

I accompanied the boat's rolling with a monotonous little inward chant. *I hate the boat. I hate the sea. I hate the fish and all marine or nearly-marine creatures, I even loathe algae. I hate the boat. I hate the sea . . .*

'I think we'll go back to port to have lunch,' my boyfriend said drily.

In my mind, the chant instantly changed. *I think we're going back to port. I think we're going back to port. I think we're going back . . .*

I didn't move a muscle of my face, though. I didn't want to make things worse for myself. But the light must have returned to my eyes, because Léon said tactfully, 'No problem. If your girlfriend thinks it's better for the children . . .'

'Yes,' I said, remorsefully stammering my apologies, 'I

think the children don't feel well. I'm sorry, Léon, you know?'

'Don't worry,' he said. 'I go sailing every day.'

'Well, that's just great,' my boyfriend burst out angrily. '*I* only get to go sailing once a year.' And he gave the tiller a sharp yank, making the poor boat, its face in the waves, whimper.

'Hey, go easy,' said his father.

'I *am* going easy,' snapped my boyfriend, chewing on his lip.

The sails began to flutter with the martial cracks of a flag being raised.

'Hold this for me and don't move, whatever you do,' said my boyfriend, jamming the tiller into my hand.

He leaped nimbly along the deck and started pulling feverishly on the first rope that came to hand. Léon threw down his dishcloth, tied his life jacket round his waist and climbed up behind him. They worked side by side, trying with all their strength to subdue the sails which were going crazy up top, dancing in the wind.

'Watch out, for goodness' sake watch out!' Léon cried to his son, who was standing in front of him, pretending he couldn't hear him.

Without looking at his father, my boyfriend came running back to me. 'Here, give me the tiller.'

I shrank sharply back in my seat as he manoeuvred. Léon watched his son with a disapproving expression. He didn't dare intervene, but he was affronted to the core of his sailor's soul.

'No,' he said, 'that's not right.'

My boyfriend shook his head without replying, distrustful, irascible, preoccupied.

'OK, that's enough. Give me that,' Léon said at last, holding his hand out.

But suddenly the wind freshened and I found myself holding the tiller again as the two men launched another attack on the rigging. The ropes flew about with a whistling sound, the winches rattled brutally and the sails cacklingly refused to submit to the wind. They flapped and sagged and shrank before its invitation.

After a while Léon moved away from the battlefield. With his hands on his hips, he observed his son. There was no longer any good nature or paternal fondness in his expression. Only total exasperation at the young Turk who was now evidently bent on sinking his boat in front of him.

'Oh, come on and give me a hand!' shouted my boyfriend. 'Don't just stand there doing nothing!'

'Why not?' said Léon, shrugging. 'You seem to be coping perfectly well on your own.'

He was sulking. But nevertheless he returned to the fray with angrily knitted brows, and after what felt like a long time the sails at last caught the wind, the hull slapped against the water with a great hiccuping noise and the boat began to pick up speed.

Father and son got to their feet and looked at one another in silence. Then Léon came up to the cockpit.

'Here you go,' he said to me softly, 'I'll take the tiller now. I'm in charge of returning to port.'

As he sat down beside me I noticed a gash on his leg.

'You've hurt yourself, Léon,' I said, pointing at the wound.

'Never mind,' he mumbled. 'It doesn't matter.'

His son came towards us, looking dishevelled, his arms hanging by his sides. He looked at his father's leg.

'Don't be ridiculous. Put something on that.'

Léon shook his head. He turned away and stared at the wave folding out from the boat.

'I'm going to get the first-aid kit from the cabin,' my boyfriend insisted.

'No,' said Léon, through clenched teeth. 'You're staying here.'

'OK, but you're being stupid.'

The pair of them fell silent, impotent and imprisoned in their rage. If a father and son want to love one another, they'd be sensible to make use of distance and caution. Because they need space in order to recognize one another, and get along. When the no-man's-land between them contracts and disintegrates, they start to chafe one another. Everything hurts, everything causes distress. No longer is it just straightforward male rivalry between them. Now it's two times fifteen tonnes of TNT waiting to blow.

And this is the point that Léon and his son had reached when I decided to step in, gaily, to try and defuse the tension.

'Perhaps two skippers is rather a lot for one boat, don't you think?'

In a way, it was neatly done. They banded together instantly and I received a unanimously murderous look.

'You just don't get it,' my boyfriend stated categorically. 'Léon is the skipper.'

Léon nodded in agreement. I slumped down in my seat and peaceably longed for the moment when I could finally set foot on firm ground.

The promise of returning had soothed my misery. All the more so because the wind had dropped, leaving only a bracing little breeze for our benefit. I wasn't completely reassured, but I felt lightened. Time, so slow and so pitiless on a boat, now had a limit. There was nothing to do but wait for our imminent return. I even found enough strength to admire the jagged rocks and vigilant pine trees guarding the shore some way off. So this is the sea wise Odysseus sailed, I thought. A few mangled Greek words came back to me, fished up from the depths of my memory. I felt almost nostalgic, as though I'd rediscovered my love of life.

'Looks like you're feeling better,' my boyfriend said, alighting like a bird at my side.

'Yes.'

And then I admitted it again and we laughed. Yes, I probably was feeling better. In the short space of a morning, I had separated from my boyfriend, lost my mind, and seen my children stretched out sick on the floor. But I had also managed a reconciliation, recovered my senses and my appetite, and watched my children bounce back, full of life. The sea, which seems so slow and so patient, makes us live at incredible speed.

'Sorry about just now,' he said. 'You know what I'm like. I've got a terrible temper and I get worked up really easily.'

'Oh no, it's my fault. I can't handle being ill. I must have been a nightmare, wasn't I?'

'Don't apologize. Next time I'll check the weather forecast and look after you a bit better.'

'*Next* time? I'm sorry to tell you that this was the last time.'

'Don't say that. It's silly. All you need is a day that's really warm and calm and . . . You'll see.'

We came into port as conquering heroes, Léon perched

jauntily in the captain's seat, holding the tiller in one hand and directing his sailor son with the other, and the two boys, back on their feet and as good as new, running around the deck and paying absolutely no attention to our warnings.

As I stepped timidly on to the quay, I felt a huge wave of relief at being back on beloved dry land. I almost knelt to kiss the ground, the good, lovely ground full of soil and pebbles.

We set up the picnic-table on the quay and were greeted by friendly calls from the occupants of neighbouring boats and the discreet 'hellos' of people strolling past.

'Sausage?' said my boyfriend.

'That was brilliant,' said my son, tipping up the mayonnaise jar on to his plate. 'Absolutely brilliant.'

3

MY COUSIN GÉRARD

LET ME tell you the story of how I, the soul of human kindness, discovered I was a nasty person. It's a true story. Could any men present please leave the room, except for family members – they can stay. Ideally, this story needs a sympathetic audience.

I wanted to leave: I'd had about all I could take with my husband. I probably could've carried on for a bit longer, but my heart was elsewhere. Not necessarily always in the same place – love comes naturally to me – but at any rate not in my kitchen. My husband's heart wasn't at home much either. But there you go, he's a man and men don't see things the same way. 'I love you, I love you,' he'd say to me, whenever seeing that I was about to leave drove him to it. It wasn't that I didn't believe him any more, I just couldn't have cared less. I'd laugh.

Everything seemed to happen quickly, but in fact several years passed before I eventually left the marital home and took shelter at my cousin Gérard's. Things fell into place by themselves. One of my brothers, who had been living at Gérard's for three or four years or more, decided to get a flat on his own. He didn't feel especially cheered by the prospect, but he hoped it might change his life. So he found a new flat, sixth floor, exposed beams. The afternoon he cleared out his stuff, I made my move. I simply asked Gérard, who dreaded being alone, if I could come and live with him. The following Monday I packed my bag, told my children what was happening and moved into Gérard's flat: the small, empty room.

I lived in that room for eight months before I threw my husband out of our house and went back home to my children. Why so long? I wonder myself sometimes. Because I was fond of Gérard, obviously; because I craved freedom; but also because I felt I was sinful, knocking over my family like skittles in one fell swoop, despite my husband's 'I love yous'.

Living at Gérard's I experienced every kind of emotion from anxiety to serenity.

'Oh, hello,' he'd say to me every evening, as if he was surprised to find me there, in his kitchen or polishing his floor. When he came home late, I'd fall asleep waiting for him, my bedroom door wide open. He wasn't working at the time – he was trying to get a job, and going slightly mad. He often went out in the evening and came home very late. He was drinking a lot. Not that I had any grounds for complaint – I was drinking pretty solidly myself, because I was tired and because of the worry of being away from my children and having to earn money for all of us.

It is a failing I have, being able to earn money. Not enough to build villas on the Riviera but enough to run a household. So when I left my home I reassured everyone: don't worry, I'll pay. And there I was, paying out left, right and centre for both flats. My husband let me – he didn't mean any harm by it, it just seemed simpler that way. Never in my life have I paid out so much.

Sometimes Gérard and I watched television, sprawled on my bed, eating pasta off his large plates and drinking cans of beer. Occasionally we asked friends round to sit in front of our little fireplace. We baked big potatoes under the logs and ate them with cream.

We fell asleep to music. Partly to make sleep come more easily, and partly, on evenings when one of us had a guest, to drown out the sound of bedsprings. We were discreet with each other. We were also anxious that the person in the other room shouldn't feel too lonely all of a sudden. In our shared living room, the CD player was the hub of the flat and proof of our consideration for others.

Neither of us remembers those months as love's finest hour. Gérard, who'd been chasing after the same woman for ten years, a tall, aloof, visionary Swede, fell into bed with various substitutes. I, on the other hand, couldn't seem to disentangle myself from the man who had been in possession of my heart for quite a while. When it began, he didn't mean any more to me than any of the others. I took him where I found him, hanging around with my brothers and my cousins. Granted, men are like wild flowers: you pick them by the wayside and everything depends on your itinerary. But one should be wary of roads used by family: because if you take your lovers too close to your siblings, there's a risk of things getting mixed up, getting too involved. But I didn't think about that at the time. As stupid as ever, I didn't imagine it lasting.

It was when I started looking at him differently, with an expression full of feeling and regret, that he ran. But ask any girl in the street, in an office, or at a dance class and she'll tell you the same story.

Let's just say he went away, he came back, he went away again and came back again, and so on. In the end my head was spinning so thoroughly that most of my time was spent waiting for him. Not that I didn't keep myself busy finding other lovers. I'm not a complete idiot. But I always ended up missing Number One. With the others, I'd be bored in the restaurant, bored on the telephone, bored even in the thick of things – in bed. There was no use pretending, I was well and truly hooked.

'My friend Didier's little sister is going to move into my flat,' he said to me one day in his kitchen, as I looked at his washing hanging over the sink.

'Right,' I answered, picking up my glass of beer and a cigarette.

'Their family's got no money, I'm helping out.'

He is a person who likes to help out, provided you don't look at him with an expression full of feeling or regret.

'Is she nice?' I asked. But I'm too old to have any illusions.

'She's just a kid, fresh-faced, level-headed, you know,' he replied, meaning to imply that her youth excluded her from being considered in a sexual light. In this he was sadly deluding himself.

He smiled as if he had the wisdom of two lifetimes, although I don't believe that any man has the capacity to remain composed for that long if you put a nice young girl in front of him. His smile was meant to convince me of the gulf between him and the girl and of the different level of respect my rank entitled me to.

I've known that smile since the day I was born. It plays me old tunes and I know the refrain. It says that the girl will be in his bed before you've had time to turn around. I'm not angry with girls, that's not the point. I'm not angry with men either, they don't realize what's happening to them. There's no use warning people, so I didn't say anything.

A fortnight later the girl was in his bed. Another day and she was going out with him in public, holding on to his arm. It was the first time he'd really gone away. I changed jobs, got bored. I won't make a big thing of the distress this event caused me. We always think we're going to die of love – me as much as anybody else, of course – but we don't.

A beautiful girl, all blonde and curvy, with notable breasts. When she chucked him, abandoned him, he came back to me – on tiptoe, but still. My sheets aren't that tightly tucked in; I took him back. It was the first time, not the last.

'Ended, it's ended,' he said.

But she didn't mark this ending by leaving his flat; having no money, she stayed to watch the parade and consequently me. I didn't say anything. I didn't want to put anyone out on the street or leave any families in need.

One evening he asked me round. I was sitting in the kitchen, in my usual place facing the washing, with a beer beside me, when the door opened and in came the girl to say hello to the grown-ups. She made her entrance completely unselfconsciously.

'Oh, let me introduce you,' he said.

He introduced us.

'Hello,' I said reservedly, mashing out my cigarette in the ashtray. Then I fell speechless. I waited for the girl to make her excuses and shut the door politely behind her, as people her age should. When she didn't, I got up, took my coat and left without saying goodbye.

That evening he stayed all alone with his girl and my beer. What's the good of me having any insight into human nature, I asked myself. With my hands in my pockets I took the Metro back to Gérard's.

'Oh, sweetheart,' said Gérard at my unexpected arrival, giving me a hug. 'Life, what a rollercoaster.'

He led me into the living room. A group of men, my brothers among them, were having supper round the table. I regarded the gathering with a certain satisfaction. With all these men around, I don't need any more, I thought to myself. I don't dislike women; I think I get on with them pretty well, actually. But I like the physical company of men, their day-to-day presence: make of that what you will.

I sat down at the table and told them of my nocturnal misadventure while Gérard rinsed a plate for me. They listened without saying anything: they all knew each other, were friends and had worked for a long time in the same type of jobs. They had all, therefore, seen the girl. They smiled demurely and I thought that they must all be remembering similar situations in which they'd played a part.

Later the phone rang for me.

'Why did you leave like that?' he asked.

How could I put it? I preferred to sleep on my own.

Every morning I got up before dawn – luckily it was

winter – and went out to earn money: phone calls, travel, meeting business contacts. In the evenings, and occasionally the mornings, I went round to my old flat to see my children, who would have tears in their eyes when I left. Then I'd go back to my room at Gérard's, lugging my bags on the Metro, tired and sad, a woman without her children. I don't hold anything against their father; after all, as my mother said, I was the one who left. Men haven't the same sense of duty. But I don't want to moan about it, it's all over now and only the memory's left.

One evening I came home to the flat, ate some pasta with Gérard, and did the washing up. Then I went and read in bed on my own. I wasn't in the mood to play the field and the person I was thinking about couldn't even be bothered to call me. Or so I thought. As my mother would say, if you go looking for trouble, you'll find it; but let's not start on all that again.

The telephone rang when I'd given up expecting it.

'Christ Almighty,' he said, before I'd even said hello.

'Alright,' I said, 'what's happened?'

I have an enquiring, maternal disposition; I'm used to people complaining.

'She's slashed her wrists,' he said. 'I've been trying to call Didier to tell him but I can't get hold of him.'

My heart started burning. A suicide: that's a big thing. I've seen them at close hand; one, in particular, broke my heart. But I was younger then and it was a man. I'm talking about suicide attempts which lead to violent deaths; in his case a gunshot in the mouth. But I mustn't dwell only on the horror stories. I've also known enough suicide attempts by young girls in the early evening, sleeping pills and stomach pumps, all so that they could go off to hospital, get between some rough sheets and receive people's condolences in person. Nevertheless I immediately thought the worst; I can't do otherwise, drama is the milk I was raised on.

'Is she dead?' I blurted.

No, she wasn't dead, and a very good thing too. So off I went, asking questions as if the girl was some underfed hamster rather than a curvy blonde who only recently had been writhing under the body of the man I loved.

Was anyone looking after her?

Were her studies going all right?

Did she have friends?

Finally I asked if I could do anything for her – discreetly. Although I was happy to help, I wasn't that keen on seeing her. It was the situation I was thinking of rather than the person.

Despite my air of laziness I love action. You admire efficiency, my mother often says when I'm tidying the kitchen. But the truth is more prosaic: so long as I'm moving, I don't think and worry passes me by. I bustled about on the phone like a squad of nuns on an Indian rubbish dump. Luckily, there was nothing I could do to help, this time: thank God. What kind of idiot would I have looked like, I ask you.

And there that story of a suicide ended; the girl took her charms off to hospital to dream in comfort, and the man hung up, about to become extremely busy telling, to his own advantage, everyone he knew. A suicide attempt by a young girl is an event destined for the front page.

Add it all together, and once again it was me who found

myself alone in bed, wide awake as if it was morning, and brought up to date to no purpose at all. Wanting to pass on the news, I got out of bed, put on my thick socks, walked across the living room and slipped into Gérard's room. He was buried under an Everest of threadbare blankets. At the foot of his bed sat an ashtray, an alarm clock and the lonely photo of his Swedish love, smiling sadly against the green backdrop of a lawn. He was leafing through a book and drinking grapefruit juice doused with gin. I sat on the edge of his mattress and lit one of his Cravens which make me cough.

'Well, guess what?' I said to him, with the expression of a Samaritan. 'The girl's tried to commit suicide.'

I was frowning. But he looked intrigued, then sat up and started laughing.

'Excellent. Let's hope she dies. We should have a drink to celebrate. Go and get yourself a glass.'

My eyes opened as wide as when I had first heard the news.

'But . . .'

'There's no buts about it,' he said. 'It's the best news we've had all week, isn't it?'

He looked at me and took my chin between his thumb and index finger, then waggled it as if to shake the worry lines out of my face. I burst into ringing laughter, like a struck champagne flute.

'She isn't dead,' I giggled.

'Pity,' he replied. 'God, she's stupid. She's so stupid. I hate her.'

My heart contracted involuntarily. 'Do you know her well?'

'Oh, there was a time,' he said obligingly, and he listed

the meetings with friends, the social events to which I hadn't been invited – out of tact – I'm not blaming anyone. As he poured out his account of the past, I suddenly realized that it was love he was talking about – one person's hand clasped in another's, in full view of everyone. What Gérard taught me then is that people always end up thrusting under your nose what you were trying your hardest to keep hidden. I felt regret bore deep into my memory.

Who were all those people who lavishly proclaimed their friendship for me yet never refused to shake hands with, or say hello to, the woman who was patently responsible for all my troubles? How simply she'd stolen all my men – and I include members of my family in that – blithely attracting them while I'd been seriously considering dying from unrequited love. Listening to my cousin relishing his memories, the feeling of being unloved gripped me again, like a cancer. No matter how much I tried to remind myself that it had just been a temporary thing, shame rose to my face. Which of the two of us women had been the most ridiculous? Be honest, it was me; history's not going to rewrite that.

'What can I say, an idiot,' Gérard concluded and handed me his half-empty glass.

Then his kind eyes fell on me and he realized that some things are better left unsaid. When he broke off, I understood that in doing so he was drawing the veil of secrecy back over a world that's too cruel. Resentment twisted inside me.

I drained the glass, imitating Gérard. I no longer felt like discussing the night-time misadventure of this person everybody seemed to know. It was clear to me now that everyone had been perfectly aware of where they'd been at certain terrible moments of my life and what they'd been doing. Time had passed since then, taking with it things as they were and as they'll remain for all eternity. I didn't say anything. For once I preferred to keep my thoughts to myself.

'Good night,' I said. 'I'm going back to bed now, I've got to go to work early tomorrow. Let's hope she'll have another go. I'm not here to make everybody happy.'

On my way past the CD player, I ran a finger over it and Nina Simone started her glorious moaning. I got in under my rumpled sheets and suddenly loneliness overwhelmed me. I cried without any pride, muffled in my unfeeling pillow. I was in full heartbreak when the phone surprised me again. I reached over to pick it up, composing myself.

'Everything's fine,' said the voice at the end of the line. 'I've managed to get in touch with Didier and her family's going to take care of it. She's out of danger.'

'Oh, that's a relief. How about you, are you all right?' I was determined to get everything back to normal as soon as possible and let the present do its repair work.

'No, I'm not OK at all,' he said, resuming his familiar litany, unconcerned by the tears that were soaking my pillow. Things were smoothly resuming their usual course.

When our nocturnal conversation came to an end, we'd made up without quarrelling, a fact that gave me more relief than pride. I had carefully crossed the Red Sea, taming its waves.

'Who was that?' shouted Gérard, when the chink of the telephone indicated the end of our endless discussion.

'Jean-Paul,' I shouted back, loud enough to drown out Nina Simone.

'And?' Gérard called.

'And, she's in hospital and everything's OK.'

'Big kiss, sleep tight Miss Right,' my cousin said as I settled down to sleep.

I mean, really, how can we be angry with these men who make up our daily lives?

But even now, on evenings when I find it hard to get to sleep, stressed out by one or other of the things that remind us we're alive, I remember that tragi-comic episode. I picture the suicide attempt and this time I add her death. With the fingers of my mind, I press on the base of her neck and wait for her to expire. I'm sorry that she didn't disappear that winter evening when, because of her, I was totally alone; far from my children and with no man to support me in my ordeal.

I wish she was dead, I repeat to myself, sitting listlessly at the kitchen table in my big flat, half-asleep. Sometimes, still, I get furious and I pray to the Lord to recall her to his side, right away if possible, if only she would just be considerate enough to attempt suicide again.

I have never stepped on a spider in my life, but I wish, unforgivingly, for the actual death of this young woman, who is like so many others, as much in her behaviour as in its consequences. Call it what you like – I think that's nastiness. I'm not proud of it, I just know it's there.

The men can come back in now. I've said what I have to say to the women and my male relations. In any case, the years have passed and, despite the ups and downs, I have achieved happiness. I don't want to lecture anyone. However, I did just want to make it clear, to those who might be interested,

that maybe I, the soul of human kindness, could kill someone one day. The thought of which fills me with joy and
makes me sparkle like the champagne in the fridge which
we are all now going to drink, if you don't mind, to my very
good health.

4

JOY

IF I heard it today, I wouldn't believe it. I'd think it was some kind of sick joke. This name: Laetitia. I'm called *Laetitia*. In English: *Joy*.

Get that: *Joy* with a capital letter. And call me Lettie. Laetitia was my mother's idea. My mother . . . That neat, severe woman, with her long skirts, her Kotex, and her scraped-back hair.

But there you go, *hic iacet lupus*. In other words: You've got to keep your eyes peeled. Like all puritans she is prone to sudden fits of over-excitement. Five hundred years ago she'd have been the sort of woman who ends up being burned at the stake after having made the whole village's life a misery. Call it what you like, the fact is, sometimes she completely loses the plot. It doesn't last long but it's pretty serious when it happens. And that day I had to bear the brunt of it.

She must have been off her head. Maybe it was the epidural. Or the emotion. Or the oxygen. But whatever it was, on that secular Whit Sunday she saw the Holy Spirit floating above the obstetrician's head, between her spread legs, and I was born in a gush of blood, fluids and Latin. At least that's my version of what happened. And if that's not how it was, explain to me how a woman who has never had anything to do with the Classics in her life just happens to receive the gift of Latin on the exact same day I was born. Let's try and be clear-headed about this. It couldn't have been down to personal resentment. Not at that stage. She didn't even know me.

My father was probably throwing up in the corridor. Giving birth's not everyone's idea of fun. Even so, the fact remains, he didn't say anything, didn't intervene in any way. Since when I've had my name. Laetitia. It's hideous, I know.

There are other calamitous names, mind you. She could have called me *Victoire*. People would've said *Vickie*. Oh, I know there are people – truly uninhibited people – who can carry off that kind of curse with style. You can see them on Saturdays in Paris, the only ones who wear riding boots to go shopping. Or those hats. You know what I mean. Velvet hats. *Victoire*. Why not *Champs Élysées*? It's also true that certain Hellenophile couplings produce offspring with absurdly Olympian handles. Why not *Marathon* . . . or even *Austerlitz*? Then I'd be *Marie. Ostie*. My God, first names, what a nightmare. Let's leave it at Lettie.

Some time after lumbering me with my ridiculous name, my mother delivered and named another child – a boy this time – whose principal aim in life was to drive me mad. Taken aback as I was by this unpleasant surprise, I did have one small cause for satisfaction. Despite the fact that she absolutely definitely can't speak a word of German, my mother called him *Wolfgang*. Wolfgang: what a stroke of inspiration! She might as well have called him Adolf. Anyway, I never address him other than with a familiar shout of *Sieg Heil!* Or, in Latin: *Vale!*

Contrary to what the above might suggest, we get on well. Relatively well, anyway. He asks me round for supper. I ask him round for supper. At supper we spend our time slagging off the few people we know. But it must be admitted that apart from these brotherly and sisterly character assassinations, our relations are fairly tenuous, even fraught, on occasion. He's jealous of me and I'm envious of him. I used to complain about him regularly to my analyst until Wolfgang started visiting him as well, on the sly. Off you go then, why don't you, all mysterious and furtive, hurrying to secretly outshine me. Three times a week at set hours of the day. It took me less than a month to find out.

'So, Wolfgang, you're giving it a go now, are you?'

Cue for him to look at the ceiling like he's drowning.

'Giving what a go, exactly, Laetitia?'

The bastard is the only person who persists in calling me Laetitia, apart from customs men and election officials.

'The couch, of course.'

He had to confess. I didn't say anything, contenting myself with directing vile curses at him through every pore of my skin. In a fit of pique, I seriously considered giving it up myself for a moment. But luckily I didn't have to resort to such extreme measures. I only had to listen to him whingeing on about it and I began to feel better. The analyst is an ass; it costs a ridiculous amount of money; and – silent session after silent session – each time he goes, poor Wolfgang feels a little unhappier. It's a sad thing to have to say but I've never heard of a cure being such a failure.

When I was very young I toyed with the idea of madness. For a while I pretended there'd been a mistake at the hospital, a baby mix-up. My parents were not my parents and my name was not my name. I became deaf to the valiant shouts of 'Laetitia'. I was distant towards my false parents and my false brother. My false parents took this pretty badly, especially when I started talking with a heavy foreign accent, keen to emphasize the mix-up. But they really lost their grip when I became an insomniac. I'd lie awake for hours desperately hoping I'd been conceived in the southern hemisphere by the Kalahari Bushmen.

'I'm going to put that little nutcase in a loony-bin!' my father would shout. He couldn't get used to my accent.

'Hear that?' my mother would whisper, complicit and afraid. 'He'll send you to the gynaecologist if you carry on your nonsense.'

Her lack of Greek meant that my mother tended to confuse gynaecologist and psychologist, women (gynae) and mind (psyche).

Eventually my father's threats subsided, and I calmed down. Not that I had found my real parents in the bush, but I had found a reason to change my behaviour. More than a reason, in fact: a method. Out of the blue my secular republican school supplied me with a worthy substitute for my efforts to disown my family. French Composition.

I abandoned my accent the day our French teacher read out my first significant essay subject in her high-pitched voice. I can still see myself, filled with emotion, writing out the title in a decorative hand, a lock of hair hanging down over my pointed face, *Describe an event which made a strong impression on you.* Made a strong impression on you: that said it all. Now it was up to me. Me, a little girl in a blue pinafore and a state of open warfare.

The French teacher was a curvy little number like a doll, all made up like the boss of a minor Civil Service department and equipped with a pneumatic body which her knitted dresses showed off to startling effect. God, what do these women get up to in their staff rooms when they're not torturing children? Get depressed, probably. Perhaps it's better not to know.

As soon as I got home I determinedly set to work, in secret, mesmerized by the title. *An event which made a strong impression on you.* We would see what we would see.

I wrote without stopping,

Forty-three days ago, the telephone rang. It was the early evening. This telephone is as black as ink and hangs on the wall in the hallway. My mother went to answer it. I was playing with my brother, Wolfgang, in the living room when we heard a piercing cry. 'No!' screamed my mother, 'oh, no!' The cry was so loud that I could almost see her, twisted over in pain, clutching her face in her hands. My father ran to her. 'What is it?' he begged, holding her in his arms. 'What is it, what's happened?' 'She's dead,' whispered my mother. 'Who?' cried my father. 'My sister,' said my mother, 'my darling sister.' Floods of tears as thick as blood streamed from her eyes, drenching her clothes. But they were only the outward signs of the wound, the sap of her heartbreak. My father rested his head on her shoulder and they stayed like that in the passage, clasped in each other's arms, as darkness fell. Two half-toppled statues, kept upright by grief alone. For an infinity Wolfgang and I remained motionless, in the middle of the living room. We had stopped breathing, perhaps to arrest the onward march of time. But we hadn't arrested anything at all. When the eternity had passed, my father came over to us. 'Your godmother is dead,' he told me. His eyes were hard and his hands hung down on either side of his body. I felt the octopus's tentacles writhe inside me. 'Dead?' I said. 'Dead,' said my father.

'I've finished my essay,' I said to my mother, when I had written the last line. 'Would you like to read it?'

'Yes,' said my mother, 'put it on the table next to the saucepans. I'll read it when I've finished straining my soup.'

Her soup! – suit yourself! I went off to my room to tend to my marigolds. I'd planted them in a plastic tub but they were refusing to flower and had produced only greenery all season. I was manhandling them ferociously when my mother summoned me.

'Lettie! Come here immediately!'

I hurtled down the stairs to receive the maternal congratulations. She was waiting for me by the telephone, as erect as the Statue of Liberty, holding my composition in her hand. Or rather, *pinching* it between her thumb and index finger as if it was a dirty little scrap of toilet paper.

'Absolutely not!' she screamed when I came down the stairs.

'Not what?' I asked.

'You have no right to write things like this!'

'Haven't I told the story well?'

'What on earth do you mean, *told the story well*?' she shrieked. 'For goodness' sake, you don't tell things like this as *stories*! You keep them to yourself, you little monster!'

At which she tore my text in two. *Rip.*

'Think of something else,' she said in a calmer voice as she studied my haggard face. 'Something normal, something nice – you know.'

'Whatever,' I said.

I went back up to my room with that bloody Wolfgang sniggering at my heels.

I spent part of the night on my second effort. But this time I didn't go and put it on the kitchen table like an idiot. I stuffed it in my schoolbag under a pile of geometry homework.

I was eight. My brother Wolfgang and I were just going to bed, when the front door slammed suddenly. From the passage at the bottom of the staircase my father called to my mother. His voice boomed as if he was furious. We came out of our room and looked down at him, him at the bottom of the stairs and us at the top, my brother and I so small in our pyjamas and my father so tall, looking up at us. His face was all smashed up, as if he had been pecked by thousands of hungry birds. But I think it was tears that had dug those grimy furrows in his face. 'What's happened?' asked my mother, standing at the door of our room, clinging tight to the banister with her delicate hand. My father came up the steps and looked at us for a moment. There was no way of knowing whether he saw victims or culprits. He just looked at us. 'Granny is dead,' he said. The sound of his words echoed in me forever, as I will forever remember the colour of the staircase's walls. Very dark red, almost black. For the first time in my child's life, I understood what death meant. It meant Never Again: never again her laugh, her face, her smell, her voice, her kiss. It meant that You will never open the door of my house again. You in your little grey twinset, your arms full of presents, your kind eyes huge behind the lenses of your glasses. I'd lost you, you in your Father Christmas outfit. My thoughts raced. The world shattered inside me. I toppled over, I felt like crying. I wanted to go back to before, before. My father couldn't do anything. He turned his back on us and went back downstairs. So I remained rooted to the spot while my mother looked after Wolfgang who'd started whimpering. I was afraid that my body would turn to stone, afraid that I'd fall to my knees and start praying to the Lord who didn't exist. Luckily the tears came and they kept me busy.

This essay was never marked because it was never handed in.

In those days my mother was going through a very active phase which involved her constantly cuffing me round the ears. My French teacher changed the style of our compositions. She suggested titles like, *A good fairy turns you into a kitten. Tell us what happens*, or *You become a toyseller. Tell us what happens.*

These idiotic subjects disgusted me but still I was always

happy to get down to them. In any case I wasn't even close to exhausting my seam. I was now composing purely for my own benefit, and reading the results to Wolfgang to make him cry.

My literary gift never bore fruit in the farcical environment of school. If anything, it damaged my capacity for social integration. In my third year, after a series of particularly inspired compositions, I was sent to the school psychologist, a short-sighted mousy woman who stank like an old grocer's. When I realized that she was never going to ask me to do anything more exciting than describe ink blots, I promised myself I'd keep my nose clean. Believe me, there's nothing more trying than having to describe an ink blot.

I graduated to secondary school. Then it became a question of pontificating about Blah-blah's love of nature or the musicality of Whodyamaflip's writing. I lost interest. I preferred maths. I didn't have much choice anyway, as I was forced to go to secondary school.

In memory of my creative years, I still filled little notebooks with furious resentment and hid them under my floorboards. When they were full, I burned them. They weren't any use to me.

Then came boys. They kept me busy in a different way and they *were* of use to me. Useful for carrying my schoolbag at the end of lessons, for example. Or for making that stupid blonde with the long limp hair and the loaded father die of jealousy.

My mother began suggesting that I was something approaching a whore (which from her implied no financial exchanges, only physical ones). The battle lines had shifted slightly. I found I was rather neglecting my writing.

One or two glorious years passed and then there I was, fifteen going on sixteen, good at equations and engaged to a number of young men, each one dumber than the last. And dreaming afresh of literary exploits. In order to return to the fray without incurring any further encounters with the school psychologist, I decided to renounce Truth and take up Art. In short, I intended to proceed undercover, and thus resume my writing with complete impunity.

To save time I took up poetry. I like quick results. After ingurgitating a considerable number of different kinds of poems, I then regurgitated them haphazardly, slyly infiltrating them with my vision. By this route I produced an endless stream of rhyming copies which – when I read them in private – made me jump for joy and pride.

For my first public reading, I decided to try my luck with a difficult audience. I chose my mother. I cornered her in the morning when she'd just got out of bed and was still eating her breakfast, munching bread and butter at the table. She gave a fearful shudder when I announced my intention to read her a poem of my own devising. But the thought of my marks in maths and physics must have reassured her and she leaned back on the kitchen bench with a victimized look. I planted myself in front of her, very upright and, with staring eyes, declaimed,

> *Wide eyes maddened eyes*
> *And the sobs that heave in their wake*
> *Along the jagged coast of my cries*

On shores that with ecstasy ache.
Ah, lost, lost, the roll of the dice
The waves on a great mirage break

Often, often, it is my dream
This friend with heavy, marbled breasts
To stroke her back with sweat agleam
Rich magic, grave bluish sex
Love with wounded lovers teems
Far, far eternity our quest

The naiads float, a hecatomb
In the rivers of our desires
In waters now, a salt black doom
A fairy moan of joy expires
Hermaphrodite hands, an icy womb
Sign where pleasure's pact requires.

I read in a clear, calm voice. And then I was quiet. I waited. There was an interminable silence. Then my mother got up from her seat, wrapped in her old pink dressing gown, a disgusted look on her face.

'Surprises will never cease,' she said in a voice that was unusually shrill, running a hand theatrically through her tousled hair. 'I wasn't aware that my daughter was a dyke.'

Misery, mistake and misinterpretation. I had prepared myself for strong reactions from my audience. But I hadn't anticipated that one.

'Would you rather I was a whore?' I said, unable to think of any better comeback yet wanting to reply with equal courtesy. I turned sharply and left the kitchen.

This experience led me to several conclusions. Firstly, I

decided to give up poetry. Secondly, I resolved to renounce the disguise of Art. And thirdly, I straight away dived headlong between the legs of my prettiest girlfriend. After all, since life is of direct use for writing, writing can also lead directly to life.

To tell the truth, it was she who suggested it, a few days after my reading to my mother. I plunged enthusiastically into her pussy, making up for any technical deficiencies with a wholly literary passion. If poetry was to bring me only one thing and if that thing was this, then long live poetry. I soon graduated from beginner to aficionado. And it seemed to me that I gave up poetry for a second time the day I realized that circumstances were pushing me predominantly towards men. But a revelation, once experienced, is never completely lost. I still have, thank goodness, that lapping ocean music of the tongue playing away in the core of my being like the onset of spring.

Some people might assume that at this point my literary vocation dried up. To think that would be to know me and my vocation very little. Admittedly, my morale had taken a terrible blow. For the remainder of my time at secondary school, I had no dealings at all, intimate or otherwise, with literary creation.

But I was to discover a new treasure trove at the point of my pencil: correspondence. And what correspondence . . . I wrote at least four or five letters every single day. Hidden away in the back row of the class, I spent all of French, History and Philosophy on them.

And, wonder of the postal system, I received almost as many letters as I wrote. Electrified by the flood of envelopes with my name on them, the postman – who was a total imbecile – christened his daughter Laetitia. At Christmas-box time he confided this with sly deference to my mother and got five hundred francs for his wretched Post Office calendar, as a reward for his servility. I wished he'd made his announcement to me. As you can probably imagine. Then I'd have liked to see him try and sell me his calendar.

Naturally my French exam for my baccalauréat was a lamentable farce. I got a six for the written paper and an eight for the oral, both over-generous considering the state of my work, which was an incoherent mess of clichés.

As a matter of interest, I'll tell you our essay subject: *Art merely creates verses; the heart alone is a poet. Explain and comment on this line of André Chénier's.*

The heart. Amusing, isn't it? Honestly, what on earth can those teachers have in their heads when they come up with that kind of title? Lead? Air? Borscht? Have these people ever written anything, even a diary, in their lives? And if so, can we read it?

For a moment I was unsure whether to come right out with my own experiences as poet. But it was the wrong time to attempt anything personal. I needed this bac to get me the hell out of my parents' house. So I mechanically churned out the required number of sentences, one after the other, on the large anonymous sheets of exam paper. When I'd finished chewing my way through the contents of the packet of sweets I'd remembered to bring with me, I had a stomach ache. I gave in my paper and ran to the toilet.

The following year, despite a shameful mark in Philosophy (I'll spare you the essay title; I seem to have forgotten it. If, that is, I ever actually read it), I got my science bac without too much difficulty. So I started medical school.

I wanted to feel people up. Medicine seemed the shortest legal route to achieving this ambition – without risking wasting my time on futile encounters, that is. I began a relentless programme of study, shutting myself away in my flea-ridden little digs and temporarily renouncing physical contact. Because before you start feeling people up, you need to know how they're made. I had my own ideas on the subject but I still had to slog away at the theory. As I discovered more and more about the unfathomable mystery of humankind and its astonishing diversity, I felt overwhelmed by emotion.

It wasn't long before this self-imposed combination of asceticism and emotion set my head spinning and brought back my old demon knocking timidly at my door. I bought a cheap notebook and got down to composing on the sly in my every spare moment. At night, lonely as an old bore, I piled up heaps of humdrum reflections as they came to me.

And sure enough, eventually the inevitable happened. Catastrophe. One morning I awoke as the author of an astounding little piece of writing. Each time I reread it, it gave me greater pleasure. I couldn't decide whether to show it to Wolfgang. He had just started a degree in archaeology, a subject chosen because he claimed to loathe the present. The little prig.

Instead, one pleasant winter's afternoon, during one of the increasingly rare meetings my parents still honoured me with, I handed my mother half-a-dozen pages torn from my notebook. I can still fondly recall her fragile maternal face falling as she read. I was sitting opposite my parents on the first floor of a large, busy café. The air smelled of beer and chocolate and I was smoking a cigarette dreamily. When my mother had turned over the last page to check there was nothing on the other side, I felt a mild twinge of satisfaction. I smiled fondly at her.

'Would you like your father to read it?' she asked, without passing comment. Her thin lips were violently pursed.

'I'd love him to,' I said.

She put the pages down on the stained table, stood up and headed towards the toilets. My father put on his glasses and held the first page in front of his nose.

'There was a first time,' my text went,

. . . a first time when, having slid my hand between my legs, my finger crossed, in astonishment, that thin boundary which separates me from the inside of myself. Until then I had been cautious, restricting myself to external contours. I dreaded breaking that little something dictionaries speak of, that temporal, resistant veil which is supposed to provide a hermetic seal between outside and inside. Not that I had considered for a minute entrusting this interesting tear to a man particularly. I don't speculate with my body. But I was afraid that in breaking the taboo I would harm myself. Complete ideological indoctrination, of course. Nothing blocked my finger's progress inside myself. Only surprise was slowing my cautious advance now. You see, I had imagined that the path to my womb was an enclosed space, one of those perpetually vacant caverns shown on anatomical diagrams. I had also imagined that it was filled with miraculously pure air, preserved immaculate in its hollow since my coming into the world.

Well, no. No little cavern or miraculous air. A soft, sticky ascent into a warm, springy canal. And all around my finger, myself. Myself spongy and wet, my own heart beating beneath my thin skin. Astonished, I hesitated to go any further. Instead I slowly withdrew my finger and brought it to my mouth . . .

'Oh, no!' my father cried, snatching off his glasses. 'That's enough!'

He threw the pages down on the table.

'But you're only on page two,' I said.

'Well, that's two pages too many,' he shouted, picking up his pipe, squinting down the stem and striking the flint of his lighter savagely.

My mother came back from the toilets, her eyes fixed on her shoes.

'Finished, darling? Shall we go?' she asked my father, without even looking at me.

'Yes,' he said nastily. 'I've had just about all I can take of this carry-on.'

He leaped to his feet. I watched as my parents grabbed their leather coats and turned their backs without even saying goodbye.

'I'll send you a cheque for the rent,' my mother called as they marched off.

But by then I was in my fourth year at medical school. I could manage without them. I picked up the beer-stained pages, folded them up and put them in my bag. A few weeks later, I lost them.

That literary encounter was the last of its kind. I haven't seen my parents much since then. They still invite me to lunch at Christmas and Easter, but I prefer to surprise them on Shrove Tuesday and the fourteenth of July. We have a convivial lunch together, then I race round to Wolfgang's to report.

My life is all I could have hoped for. I've been a practising gynaecologist for ten years now and in my professional capacity I get to feel up a tremendous number of people, especially women. In my professional capacity I also lament the fact that men don't take better care of their women. If they devoted only a tenth of the time they spend drinking or pretending to work to looking out for them, the world wouldn't be how it is. Sometimes I think of those American scientists who study the sensitivity of plants by attaching great electrodes to the plant's veins. I picture them returning home in the evening after a day of plant sensitivity. Which of them marvels at the thin web of veins and fine lines stretched over his wife's body? Which of them monitors her capacity to react to emotional shocks? I don't want to sound accusatory, but, believe me, women have at least as many sensors as begonias. And it's about time people paid more attention to them.

I write articles regularly for the *International Review of Gynaecology*. I stuff them with digressions which disappear from the published versions. But I'm not offended by people's fondness for censorship.

The truth is, I'm waiting impatiently for May. On the seventh of that month, a wonderful crowd of strangers will be able to buy in their usual bookshops – perhaps even at their newsagents' – an appealing little work written by me. Here's a sneak preview: the title is: *My Parents, Wolfgang and Me: from single partners to multiple partners, the emotional and sexual life of a French family from the sixties to the eighties*, by Laetitia Lerousseau. I'm sure this first book of mine will make its mark, if not in the history of literature then at least in that of the human sciences. At any rate my publisher seems very confident about its public reception. He's given it a four-colour jacket on glossy paper. My photograph takes up about half the cover. I wonder what they're all going to think. It's going to be a real surprise.

5

SOMETHING'S WRONG

RÉMI WAS already very busy at work at the time of the move.

'You mustn't count on me being around much for, maybe, six to ten months,' he warned Agnès when he asked her to come and live with him.

'I'm used to living by myself,' Agnès replied. 'I don't mind waiting for you.'

At the beginning of August, Agnès hired a removal firm. Her brother offered to help keep an eye on proceedings and she accepted gratefully. On the Friday evening before the move, she began to pack her belongings into boxes. With a thick black felt tip, she wrote 'ODDS AND ENDS' on half of the boxes, and 'REST' on the others. She spent a good part of the night separating the past from the future. What she didn't jam into the boxes, she stuffed into rubbish bags, which she carried downstairs and put out on the pavement.

The next morning, two hulking youths and a small, lazy-looking man with a moustache turned up at the flat, which seemed strangely airy and inviting because of the stacks of boxes. After a cup of coffee and a few routine jokes, they loaded up the van. Then, at around midday, Agnès got in and they drove the three kilometres separating the old flat from the new one. As she left the place she'd lived in for the past two years, Agnès didn't look back once at the empty rooms, which at that time of the day were bathed in vast pools of sunlight.

She had brought beers and grapefruit juice, fearing that hauling her possessions up to the fourth floor would be a long job. But it proved relatively easy. As soon as the men left, in the early afternoon, she realized that she had turned Rémi's melancholy, peaceful flat into a chaotic, depressing warehouse. I can't wait for it to be repainted, she thought. She turned towards her brother who was sitting on a bench in the middle of the mounds of stuff, recovering. She hoped he'd suggest they have supper together. He said he'd love to stay, but he had to be somewhere else. So she shut the door behind him, lay on the bed and cried.

'So,' her best friend said to her on the telephone that same evening, 'this is it. You've moved. You're living together now. Who would've guessed it six months ago. And now it's happened. You must be so happy. I'm so pleased for you. It's fantastic.'

'Yes, it's fantastic,' said Agnès.

Lying down in the little bedroom filled with rows of shoes and piles of clothes, she flicked through *Le Monde* and listened distractedly to the predictable string of questions.

'What are you doing this evening?' Nathalie asked. 'I've asked some friends round, they're musicians. You'd really like them. Do you want to come over?'

'No, thanks, you're a sweetheart,' Agnès said. 'But I've got a dinner that was arranged ages ago. I can't get out of it. I'll call you tomorrow, if you like.'

She put the phone down and picked up the *Pariscope* lying at the foot of the bed. She looked for a cinema in a well-lit part of town – on the Champs, say, or in the Fifth. She dreaded going out alone at night to somewhere dark and deserted, somewhere as sad as she felt.

Flats come together gradually – everyone knows that. So Agnès started slowly, unable to distribute things harmoniously about a space which was now cluttered with paint pots and workmen's ladders. She repeatedly moved the cardboard boxes from one end of the flat to the other, bracing herself to drag the heavy masses across the parquet floor, straining to carry weights she wasn't used to.

'I'm not managing very well,' she'd confess with muffled despair when she saw her friends.

'It's normal, it takes time to do up a flat,' the friends would reply, smiling. 'Everything'll be great in a few weeks.'

But Agnès knew very well that it wasn't normal. And she couldn't envisage anything great in the weeks to come either – nothing whatsoever. She also realized that her friends couldn't do anything to help her any more, now that she'd moved, and everything was fine.

Despite their frequent absences, the workmen Agnès had employed finished painting the half of the room she'd assigned to them. She wrote out a cheque to the eldest and watched with relief as they packed up.

Then she appraised the furniture with a feeling of helplessness. She slid it across the floor, to the right and then to the left, then put it back to how it had been previously. She gave up on hanging the pictures and left them leaning against the skirting board. Then she lost interest in the reception rooms. She stopped going into them except to use the stereo or watch the television.

She decided to paint the big room that was going to be her and Rémi's bedroom herself. At last, the sort of job that suited her. Lay the groundsheets out on the floor, sponge down the walls with big sweeps of the arm, climb the ladder – and paint until your hands are blistered, your arms ache and your neck is stiff.

She had estimated it would take three days. It took more than a week and twice she had to go out and buy more paint. After the third day, she didn't want to look at herself in the mirror any more and she decided to stop washing her hair. She hated herself. Nevertheless, she saw it through, her arms crooked with cramp. All day long she thought of the bit in *The Baker's Dozen* where little Mark volunteers to paint his father's garden fence for one measly dollar. At the end of the story, impressed by his son's perseverance, his father gives him ten dollars. *Ten dollars*, she repeated to herself, as the roller spat a shower of white droplets into her face.

When she had finally moved the bed into a corner of the room, she felt a sense of achievement. Exhausted by the effort of carrying the two mattresses from one room to the other, she fell asleep serenely, her hair washed, before Rémi came home from work.

Autumn came and Rémi spent more and more time at work. Agnès loved waiting for him, pretending not to care, lying on the floor in front of the television.

'Back already?' she'd say, looking at him with affectionate eyes when he pushed open the door, usually in the middle of the night.

They'd have coffee together, or vodka, sitting next to each other in the cluttered kitchen.

'What have you done today?' Rémi would ask mechanically, rubbing his eyes with the back of his hand.

'Oh, nothing special,' Agnès would answer. 'How about you?'

'The usual,' Rémi would say.

And they'd go to bed. She was silently delighted to see him come back, night after night, and fall asleep next to her, his hand on her thigh.

Apart from waiting, she spent part of her time working, proofing galleys in the back rooms of printers. She moved around regularly, as the work came in. She didn't take much interest or trouble in the job as she had no particular liking for it; she'd always been good at spelling, and able to apply herself conscientiously, anyway. But she felt comfortable in the masculine, hard-working atmosphere of the printers. She was impressed by the typographers' tattoos and joined them in lamenting the irreversible decline of their profession.

The rest of the time she divided between her friends, slipping from one to the other with the bitter sense that she was fulfilling an urban duty rather than an emotional desire. Her friends loved her companionableness and were grateful to her for being a good storyteller. As for Agnès, she was always amazed and thrilled at being able to make people laugh.

When she got back to the flat at night, she was at last free to return to her personal concerns. She'd lie down in front of the television and wait for him.

'I'm happy, very happy,' she whispered in Rémi's ear sometimes, after they'd made love and were slipping down the implacable slope of sleep. These few words would arouse in her a formless, heart-rending feeling of regret, and the disastrous temptation to start crying. So she'd fall asleep quickly and dream about dying.

Since he'd asked her to move into his flat, Rémi had seemed content. It wasn't that he showed any particular satisfaction with the arrangement, he had never been one for making declarations. But he was good-tempered and proved himself most of the time to be more attentive than his smiling silences might have suggested.

'What's worrying you?' he'd ask regularly, with no symptoms to go on other than her distracted expression. 'Everything's fine.' And he'd put his hand on her leg.

For a man who prided himself on his independence and his fondness for women, Agnès's visible inclusion in his everyday life represented a supreme display of affection. Sometimes he himself would marvel out loud at the fact that he'd asked her to move in.

'It's the first time I've actually made the decision,' he'd say. 'Before now, living together was always something that was forced on me.'

Agnès made do with this largesse. After all, she loved him, and had done so for a long time. And day by day they were proving to each other that they were made to be together.

When the kitchen and bathroom were finished, Agnès felt at a loose end.

'Don't you think it's strange that we never talk about your past?' she asked one evening just after they'd switched out the light.

Rémi sighed.

'But we have, haven't we?'

Agnès persisted, determined to lift up the paving stone even if it meant a swarm of black cockroaches scuttling out.

'Yes,' she replied, 'we have, once or twice, about your childhood. But I wanted to talk about our past as adults – our recent past.'

Rémi turned over to face the wall, taking most of the duvet with him.

'What would be the point?' he mumbled. 'If something's bothering you, you've only got to ask me specific questions and I'll answer them.'

'Oh, I wasn't thinking of anything specifically,' Agnès said, confused. She moved closer to him and tugged at the duvet. 'But often, to get to know each other – or when they know each other better – people talk about their lives. They share their memories. They tame each other, if you see what I mean.'

'Well,' said Rémi firmly, 'I'm not like that. I can't think of anything to tell you about the past. It's all ancient history, anyway . . . and it's hardly uplifting.'

'So you think people have to live in the present, is that it?' Agnès asked obstinately.

'Yes, if you like.'

'And you think that you can live in the present without the past?'

'Yes,' said Rémi.

'Is this your attitude to your whole life, or just to our life together?'

'I'm tired,' Rémi said. 'You're confusing me. Let's talk

about this later when I'm not so busy at work. For now, why don't you stop torturing yourself with pointless questions? After all, you're here, in this bed, aren't you? Your name's on the letter box, isn't it? What more do you want?'

'True,' said Agnès.

After he'd gone to sleep, she thought about the other names she'd seen on the letter box in the three years before she'd moved in.

Winter drew closer and with it the urge to hibernate. Agnès was anxious to get the flat finished as quickly as possible.

'Tomorrow I'm going to clear out your little room and finish moving us into the big room,' she said to Rémi one night before they went to sleep.

'Good idea, then we'll be able to convert the study. We should get a sofabed and make it a guest room.'

'OK.'

'I'm working too much,' Rémi grumbled. 'I'm sorry all this is getting dumped on you.'

'Don't blame yourself,' said Agnès. 'It's fair enough. You'll concentrate on us when you've finished your work.'

'You're so lovely,' said Rémi, checking that the alarm clock on the bedside table was set.

The next morning Agnès set off in warm autumn sunshine to buy two big boxes and six small ones. She was going to clear out the cupboards, then pack Rémi's things away until he had time to sort them out. She came back to the flat at about midday and made herself a cup of coffee, which she drank calmly, listening to the radio. Then she started on the changeover.

It's difficult to touch the physical evidence of someone else's past. You can put on gloves to protect your hands, but you can't wear a mask to shield your eyes. Agnès decided to start with the study. She stacked up the layers of papers on and around Rémi's desk, and fed them into the gaping mouth of the box, filling the gaps in between with tightly rolled posters and ancient diaries.

As she worked, odd items caught her gaze. She held them between her fingertips and shook the dust off them. Trifles that appeared to have been kept deliberately she slipped into thick plastic pouches. She too had once owned outdated bits and bobs like these, old postcards, shells – those worn and rusty charms which one finds it difficult to part from and keeps like a hardened foam of memory. It's left to time to take them away. Or moving house. She felt embarrassed being so close to the material contours of Rémi's past and stuffed his things into the cardboard box with an uneasy conscience.

She carried the first big box into the new bedroom and pushed it under a table. Then she brought in two saucers, each filled to the brim with minute souvenirs which had floated to the surface of the sentimental hoard. She laid them on the desk and blew off the uniform coating of dust.

In one of the saucers there was a card. She looked at it for a moment. It was a pass issued by a ski resort for a day on the slopes. In the little photo Rémi looked his usual self, but his face was rested, his skin smooth and tanned and you could see the collar of his anorak. To Agnès, who had never skied, he seemed as remote as an anonymous photo on the travel pages of a magazine under the headline 'WINTER BREAKS'.

She tackled the cupboard. She opened her second big box and wedged sets of old magazines into the bottom.

Then she filled the cracks with various feminine objects, the survivors of old shipwrecks – necklaces which were no longer in fashion, flat shoes, bracelets.

Only a series of shallow boxes bearing the logo of an American shirtmaker were left. The first felt light; she opened it; it was empty. She put it to one side to be added to the bags she was going to carry down and put out on the pavement. The second contained letters. She recognized her cramped writing with its precise downstrokes on the envelopes that had been tossed in haphazardly. Oh wow, she thought. She sat down and opened one. The pages still showed the fold line after she'd smoothed them out. She glanced through these fragments of her past with curiosity, but, gnawed by a feeling of shame, quickly gave up reading them. She folded the pages and slipped them back into the envelope.

Under the first letter, there were other letters of hers. Other pieces of paper as well, meticulously kept, chance messages written at meetings and farewells, the kind of hurried, affectionate notes you leave on the fridge or slip under a door. Among them, an evasive card posted from a place she had never set foot in. The card may have been signed with the same first name, but the rounded handwriting wasn't hers. The charm of collections lies in their flaws, thought Agnès, the golden beetle pinned in the middle of the butterflies.

Under the carpet of her envelopes were other envelopes addressed by a different hand. She turned one over. On the back she read the correspondent's first name. Her letters were also filed away, along with her bare, informal little missives.

Agnès was seized by a curious wave of sisterhood for her storage companion. The sisterhood Bluebeard's wives must have felt when they were finally reunited in their narrow cupboard, randomly lined up next to each other, their long dresses equally spattered with black blood.

Finally she reached the bottom of the box, a light, oatmeal-coloured cardboard which felt soft to touch.

The other boxes were similarly filled with communications sorted by handwriting. A quick rifle through with her fingertips allowed her to work out how many. Being all the same format, the boxes were admirably suited to being stacked on top of each other. Agnès kept aside the box she shared and put it on top of the pile. Then she closed the big box and dragged it to the new bedroom, where she slid it under the table next to the first one.

She filled the small boxes with what was left on the shelves and put them on top of the big ones. Then she wedged her cardboard edifice against the wall and went and washed the dust off her hands.

There we are, she thought, that's one thing out of the way. Now we've got a guest room.

Coming back into the bedroom, she picked the ski pass off the floor at the foot of the desk. But when she was about to return it to the saucer, she noticed it didn't have the same photo. It must have fallen out of one of the small boxes. Instead of Rémi there was a fresh-faced young woman with brown hair and regular features. Agnès compared the dates on the two cards, then she read the name. She studied the face more closely. Ah, she thought, it's her. For a moment she was tempted to put the card next to Rémi's, two vignettes displayed in a prominent place on the desk, not to embarrass him but to reunite two small chipped pieces of his universe. Instead she slipped the pass into the box, and the little photo went back down into the impregnable hold of the recent past.

That evening she didn't answer the phone when it rang. She dreaded the caller hanging up at the sound of her voice. A few days earlier, whilst they'd been drinking tea in the kitchen, she had complained to Rémi about these anonymous calls. He had shrugged and she'd been left with the unpleasant feeling of being silly. Something's wrong, she thought when they'd gone to bed.

'Do you want me to leave?' she asked Rémi before he went to sleep.

'No, why, are you crazy?' he said.

She decided not to pick up the phone any more, preferring that Rémi's callers rang him at work. She got into the habit of ringing people back if they left a message; anyway, she'd never been all that keen on talking on the phone or obeying its tyrannical ringing.

'What?' one of her girlfriends had exclaimed when she moved in. 'You're going to have the same phone number?'

Agnès hated the forced, fake-astonished tone of the question.

'Of course,' she replied curtly, 'seeing as we're going to be living together. I can't imagine what a life with two lines would be like. I'd rather live in a hotel.'

A few days after this conversation she'd examined the reasons for her friendship with this young woman.

Too much wasted time, she'd decided, I can't love everyone on the planet. And she'd broken it off there.

The next day, as she contemplated the new bedroom in the

dusk, Agnès's teeth started chattering.

'I feel anxious,' she told her brother, who had rung up to see how she was getting on.

'Do you want me to come round after supper?' he suggested.

'No thanks, I think I've got to get used to coping on my own,' Agnès said.

She went into the living room and lay down in front of the television with a glass in her hand. But despite switching from one channel to the next, she couldn't shrug off the feeling that the flat was breathing to its own, autonomous, hostile rhythm. The vivid little images danced in the narrow frame of the set but she couldn't see anything except a fog of colours.

She stood back up and went into the kitchen to have a look at the clock. It was barely ten. Rémi wouldn't be back before three or four.

'I think I'm not well,' Agnès said, addressing the empty flat in a low voice. 'Three or four o'clock, that's too long.'

When she picked up the phone to dial the number, her heart was racing like an express train. Fred, who rarely went out before midnight, picked up on the second ring.

'Fred?' said Agnès.

'Agnès, what a lovely surprise,' said Fred.

'Are you doing anything this evening?'

'I don't know yet. Shall we go and have a drink?'

'Now?'

'Yes, of course now. Why wait?'

In the street, as she looked for a taxi, Agnès noticed that her heart had suddenly quietened down. She touched her chest with her hand. Her heart was beating imperceptibly, calmly, reassured. Like her it was always happy to leave their stifling home and slip into the open air, into the welcoming, animated night.

'Well,' she said, when Fred was sitting in front of her, still wearing his big black coat, 'I'm very happy to see you.'

Fred took her hands over the café table and kissed them. He kept his eyes on her, scrutinizing her face.

'So why don't you more often, then?' he asked, imprisoning Agnès's hands in his.

She was dazed by the racket of the surrounding tables, the cigarette smoke and the waiters' bustle. Her eyes shone.

'Because we've split up, if I could just refresh your memory.'

'Yes. So?' said Fred. 'I don't see what difference that makes.'

He pushed himself quickly up from his seat to take off his coat, almost bumping into the waiter who put two glasses of beer down in front of them.

'It's because of the guy you live with, isn't it?'

'Yes,' said Agnès.

'Does he make you happy?'

'Oh, he's very kind. As for me being happy, well, that's up to me, don't you think?'

Fred shook his head doubtfully. Then he stood up again and leaned forward to whisper in Agnès's ear.

'Do you make love often enough?' he said.

Agnès jerked her head away.

'What an idiotic question,' she said. 'Exactly the sort of question I never answer.'

'Fine, fine,' said Fred, sitting down again, 'never mind. But I don't have much confidence that he's making you happy. You know that, don't you?'

'Please,' said Agnès, 'don't tell me. You know too many people and you know too much about them. Can each of us keep our secrets to ourselves, please.'

'Still, I'd love to mess things up for him,' remarked Fred.

'No,' said Agnès, 'you'd mess me up at the same time.'

'I'd never do that, angel. Now, why don't you tell me why you're calling me in that husky voice in the middle of the night?'

'It's because I don't understand men. You've got to explain them to me.'

In meticulous detail, she told Fred about the evenings spent waiting, the accumulation of small anxieties. Fred listened, from time to time putting his hands on her wrists or on her knees. He was tall and brown-haired and looked a little like Agnès's first husband – a younger, cockier version with straight hair. They both had the same selfish gift for happiness. When Agnès, after the enchantment of discovery had worn off, had realized the profound similarities between Fred and his predecessor, she knew sadly that she would never love him.

'So, what do you think?' she asked, when she had finished her beer and her account of her daily life. 'Do you think I'm just making up things to worry about?'

'I think you haven't got any common sense,' said Fred. 'We're old now, Agnès. We're old, fragile, brittle things, worn by life. We should treat one another gently and keep our distances. So be reasonable; you should take him as he is, absences and silences included. You need time to judge someone, and the more the years pass the more time you need. That's what I would have asked of you if we'd lived together.'

'For goodness' sake, what's that got to do with anything? You share your life the way people share bread, everyone just grabbing handfuls. You talk so much that sometimes I'd prefer it if you kept quiet. And you're always there when I call you.'

'Yes,' said Fred, 'but you don't call me often. And I'm not the one you've chosen to live with. He is. So you've got to learn to work it out with him.'

'Great,' said Agnès, crestfallen, 'it sounds as though you're giving me a lecture.'

'Every dog has his day,' said Fred, recovering his smile. 'So, now tell me, when are you going to cheat on him?'

'Are you kidding?'

The waiters started stacking the chairs on the tables. Then half the lights went out at once. There were only a few couples left, chained to their tables.

'I've got to go home,' she said.

'OK,' said Fred. 'Let's go.'

He went with her to the taxi rank. They walked side by side in the cold.

'Everything would be much simpler if you decided to love me,' he said placidly as he strode along, hands buried deep in his pockets.

'What do you know?' she asked, glued to his side by the cold and the rhythm of their walking. 'It's because we were just lovers that everything's fine between us.'

'But we could have stayed lovers all our lives,' said Fred. 'We'd be very happy.'

'It's impossible,' said Agnès. 'You know that. One day you'll want to live with someone as well, be there when they're asleep and when they wake up, and feel the weight of the tie that binds you securely together.'

When she was sitting in the taxi, he bent down to kiss her.

'Call whenever you want,' said Fred, shutting the door of the taxi gently. 'But don't ask my advice too often. I won't always have the patience to send you back to someone else.'

The next night Agnès's mother came for supper after spending the day in Paris. Rémi joined them for pudding.

As soon as they'd finished, Agnès's mother said, 'I have to go, darling.'

'Are you sure you want to go back this evening?' asked Agnès. 'You can sleep here and then go home tomorrow without having to rush.'

'Oh no.' Her mother smiled. 'I'd rather sleep at home, with your father, and get up late tomorrow. Would one of you be kind enough to put me on the right road? I can never find the slip road on to the motorway.'

'I'll come with you,' said Rémi. 'It'd be a pleasure.'

'That's very sweet of you, Rémi. I'm going to kidnap him for half an hour,' she said, turning to Agnès. 'Don't be too angry with me. And thank you for a lovely evening.'

When she had closed the door behind them, Agnès cleared the table and did the washing up. She was shaking the tablecloth out of the window when the phone rang. She picked it up quickly.

'Hello. Agnès?' said Rémi. 'I've met some friends on the *périphérique*. They've asked me to a party.'

'You met some friends on the *périphérique*?' asked Agnès, repeating each syllable carefully.

'Yes, just now, I bumped into them. I'm just going to have a drink with them and then I'll come back.'

'OK,' said Agnès, mechanically.

'Is anything wrong?' asked Rémi.

'No, everything's fine.'

'OK, see you soon.'

'See you soon,' said Agnès, looking at the time. It was one o'clock. She put down the receiver.

Stupid, she thought. No one bumps into friends on the *périphérique* at one o'clock in the morning.

Her heart was pounding like a bombardment again. She thought about going out like before into the welcoming night to calm it. But she was too tired to call her brother and she was afraid of hurting Fred. So she got a strip of sleeping pills out of the bathroom cupboard and popped out a pill which she swallowed when she was in bed.

I'll see tomorrow, she thought, sinking down into the darkness.

Protected by the layers of sleep, she didn't hear Rémi come home.

Next morning she woke up to the sound of the radio blaring in the bathroom. Rémi was in the shower. She went into the kitchen and made coffee.

'Morning,' said Rémi, coming out of the bathroom. 'What's new?'

'Oh, nothing special,' she said, sitting down. 'How about you?'

'Nothing,' he said, wiping his face. 'I'm hideously late.'

She poured herself a full cup of coffee. She avoided looking at Rémi, who was getting ready to leave.

'Do you want a cup of coffee before you go?'

'No time,' said Rémi.

He poured aftershave into his cupped hands.

'I've got to run. I'm sorry, everything will be better when I finish this job. Just be patient a little longer.'

'Well, bye then,' she said, 'good luck.'

She walked to the door with him. He kissed her. She watched him rushing down the stairs, slipping on his jacket.

In the kitchen she sat back down and slowly drank her coffee and smoked a cigarette.

'I'm sick of this,' she said to the flat.

She had a bath and put on warm clothes. Winter had come. It was night now all day long.

She went into the bedroom and from the big box gathering dust under the desk took out the small box at the top of the pile. She extracted her letters and messages, identifying them by the handwriting. Then she carried the slim bundle over to the fireplace, struck a match and set it on fire. The letters burned together, throwing up multi-coloured flames brightened by a few photos. She crouched in front of the fireplace, watching the short-lived fire and the filmy ashes dancing in the updraught. When the last embers had gone out, she put the fireguard back.

She went back into the bedroom and filled her travel bag with her everyday clothes and her washing things. She sat down at the kitchen table and tried vainly to write a farewell note. After she'd written 'Dear Rémi' and then torn up the piece of paper three times, she gave up.

I can't write to him, she thought as she stood up and picked up her travel bag. Anyway he'll see I'm not here any more.

I'd better think about calling a removal firm, she thought as she shut the door of the flat behind her. Then she went out into the chilly, lively street and began looking for a hotel.

*

'I don't believe it,' her best friend said when Agnès phoned that same evening. 'Are you sure you haven't done something stupid?'

'Who knows?' Agnès replied. Lying on the bed with its firmly tucked sheets, she was idly scanning the list of services offered by the hotel. 'Maybe.'

'Maybe you should call him and sort this thing out,' Nathalie insisted. 'It's stupid, isn't it?'

'There's nothing to sort out,' said Agnès. 'It's too late.'

'Well, then, come and have supper tomorrow evening. I've asked some friends round, some painters. You'd really like them. We can talk about this properly then.'

'OK, great,' said Agnès. 'I've got to start looking for a flat too.'

'OK,' said Nathalie. 'I'll see you tomorrow. And don't think twice about calling me, whatever the time, if anything's wrong.'

Agnès put the phone down. She picked up the remote control and turned on the television. She bunched the pillows at the head of the bed and settled down comfortably, facing the screen, her address book within easy reach.

6

HAIKU

MY LIFE changed the day my friend Anne-Lise introduced me to haikus. Say *Hi*, as if you're rushing madly towards a friend you haven't seen for ages. And *Coo*, as if you're imitating the last sigh of a dove whose neck you've just wrung. *Hi-Coo*. It's Japanese.

Yes, one day my life changed. You can pause for a minute and dream. Because we all dream, don't we, that one day the wretched merry-go-round that some of us call 'my life' will stop. We dream of climbing down from the painted pig that's our mount and heading off, calm, alone, towards the Other Life. But look around; not many people manage it. Because the merry-go-round never stops. You have to jump off while it's still moving.

So. I owe my discovery of haikus to Anne-Lise. Anne-Lise is capable of doing a great deal of good. Not that she sets about it in a straightforward manner, that's not her way. She has neither a great heart nor a noble soul. She might even be taken for selfish and petty-minded.

Anne-Lise is like life. Unconsciously she generates a

pointless, constant ferment. All it takes is a spark and some marvel emerges. For instance, she's interested in a considerable number of things. You might even go so far as to say that she changes her interests as often as her shirt. One day it's interior design, the next Indian philosophy, the next sailing lessons organized by the Union Nationale des Centres Sportifs de Plein Air. I'm not saying that all of this is equally interesting. But sometimes, *sometimes*, my friendship with her is rewarded beyond my wildest dreams.

But let's start at the very beginning, at the exact moment when fate threw me a rope and I grabbed hold of it. We were having lunch in the Grand Café. We used to meet up like this regularly, like accomplices, to assess the Latest News in our lives. Of course this air of complicity was a sour illusion. Anne-Lise may have been brimming over with outrageous new anecdotes all the time but I had to listen to morning radio to have any idea of what the Latest News might be. At the time my life was pretty much like a canal. Slow, glassy and dark.

How little we know our own lives. I didn't think of myself as unhappy. I thought I possessed the majority of those attributes which guarantee an individual access to happiness. I liked going out, for example. On good days, I could pass for a sociable, even a funny person. I had quite a few friends. Together we expended a lot of energy on activities of an entertaining kind – dinner parties, films, picnics – skiing holidays, even. I had stuck up photos of this merry band on the walls of my flat: smiling girls, dreamy boys. That way, I could see with my own eyes that the awful feeling of loneliness which sometimes brought me to my knees was the result of a calcium deficiency rather than a warning given free of charge by a heart suffocating from boredom.

I spent the greater part of my time working, incidentally. I was the Girl Friday at Global Promotions, a small firm that produced everything from books to T-shirts, magazines to music, club nights to invitation cards. Of course if you involve yourself in everything, nothing you do is likely to be all that brilliant. But you get to do interesting things, you have a good time, you make friends. That's where I met Anne-Lise, for example, only a few months before she resigned. I was captivated by her energy, and by the amazing number of young people who seemed to be attracted to her cluttered office.

I spent most of my days physically trapped between a telephone, a fax machine and banks of files. Tucked away in my little office, I'd watch a lot of interesting people come and go – journalists, photographers, graphic designers, multimedia types. I liked all these creative people, but I didn't envy them. At the end of each job, when I held the fruits of their labours in my hand – a book, a magazine, a printed polo shirt or a video – I'd feel a slight sense of desolation on their behalf. I preferred my warm, unassuming place. At least I always had plenty to do there and never had to compromise myself.

So my life was quiet and well-organized. Sometimes, though, in the night, I'd be overtaken by an attack of breathlessness. A kind of fit which would suddenly seize me viciously, taking my breath away for hours and leaving me exhausted and tearful in the morning. I dreaded these episodes and complained about them. But curiously, I also anticipated them with a kind of agitated hopefulness. I loved the pallor they left me with the next day, the delicate haloes they etched round my eyes. Eventually I convinced myself that I was asthmatic and decided to have a check-up.

The doctor examined me with a stethoscope for a long time, tapping me gravely on the back, making me breathe in and out, cough, spit. Then he took off his maroon cardigan and stubbed out his cigarette self-importantly.

'Well, my dear,' he said, 'it's time you took a little holiday.'

'So I'm not asthmatic?' I said, ruefully.

The doctor shook his head with a little smile. He sucked his pencil.

'Spasmophilic, possibly,' he said, tearing off a prescription from his pad. 'We'll put you on a long course of homeopathic medicine. And I'm also going to prescribe tranquillizers which you're to take at the start of every attack.'

Placebos and sleeping pills. It was like a cruel summary of my life. And you can't take medicine for your life. I let the prescription curl up on the corner of my desk.

At times I'd gladly have exchanged my quiet existence for something more eventful. Something more romantic, say. To be honest, what I was missing was a man. I wondered what their secret was – those girls who managed to find a lover on every street corner. Which streets were they exactly? If I tramped through the whole of Paris and strained my eyes at the smallest crossroads, I still couldn't see anything.

I have to admit that it's also a matter of choice. I'm not

the sort to throw myself on the neck of the first offer that comes through the door of my office. Of course, sometimes, at the end of a party, I'd let myself drop into the arms of a stranger who was half-drunk or completely insane. But tell me, how can anyone be satisfied with that sort of situation? Personally, I thought that things should have a certain grandeur, if only to compensate for the pain they end up causing. But a sozzled or clinically insane stranger rarely gives you that dizzying feeling. They're more likely to leave you flat – or sometimes even totally buried under the sand, squashed like a melancholy flounder.

After a while, I gave up on affairs. You get used to sleeping alone. I made do with daydreaming. My wandering, sentimental thoughts regularly latched on to tall men with promising smiles, like those who rushed in and out of my office, taking or handing over orders, trailing smells of grass and aftershave. Before they'd even turned and walked away, my heart would have done a somersault. All day long, memory would do its work on them and imagination its embroidery. First date, first kiss, first argument – I'd tell myself, in infinite detail, the story that would bring us together.

Then I'd discover from Anne-Lise that she'd just spent the night with my imagined companion. I came to dread the implacable ring of the phone, the moment I'd fallen for someone, bringing me back to reality. 'Anne-Lise?' I'd say.

'Yes, it's me,' her voice would shrill into my ear. 'Guess where I've just come from? Guess!'

She'd just come from Christophe, Alain or Matthieu's bed, as I knew only too well.

Eventually I came up with a philosophy. I'd look at myself in the bathroom mirror in the morning, as naked as God made me, and think: Better one true love than ten squalid little flings. Loving, sentimental and old-fashioned: that was me. I began to think that the good Lord had picked the wrong era when he'd hurled me to earth. I'd have liked to have been born a century earlier, when women still had a value and men still had feelings. But what difference did the good Lord, fashion and regrets make? The upshot of it all was this: my cat was the only living creature sharing my flat. And I hadn't even asked for his advice. Despite my newly philosophical outlook, I still ended up giving him filthy looks.

But let's go back to Anne-Lise. Most of the time she's a charming girl, but she can also be a complete cow. Spoilt people sometimes lose their sense of proportion. It has to be said that she is really pretty. She has a large, very sensual mouth and wide blue eyes, which she can narrow into slits, which serve simultaneously as passport and absolution. Everything in her life happens as if heaven itself finds it difficult to refuse her the smallest thing. And I'm not just talking about men here. They fall over each other for the pleasure of being trampled in the mud by her patent-leather ankle-boots.

We had barely sat down at our little round table before she started, nonchalantly flicking her blonde hair and pouting her full lips, 'So, Christiane, what's new?'

She caught me off-guard, just as I was calmly gearing myself up to endure another detailed account of her action-packed life. I tried to think. My memory echoed hollowly like the shell of a sucked egg.

'Nothing,' I confessed, finally. 'No, there's really nothing new to report.'

Anne-Lise leaned nervily over the table to scratch her ankle. She looked furious.

'For heaven's sake, Christiane, you've got to try a little bit harder. Nothing ever happens to you. Make a bit of an effort, for goodness' sake.'

'That's easy for you to say,' I said, with a hint of bitterness. 'What do you suggest?'

'Well, I don't know . . . You could change jobs, for a start. At least that would be a step in the right direction.'

This is what she coolly instructed me – when I'm the one who's supposed to be so calm and well paid, whilst she's so badly paid she's been trying to leave her job in advertising for the past three years. For a second I felt like crying. I hadn't even taken my coat off and already I had to start justifying myself, when all I'd hoped for was an amusing little interlude. I felt horribly disappointed.

'There's no need to be unpleasant,' I said, stoically crushing my coat against the back of my chair. 'I've got lots of plans. I'm thinking of taking quite a big trip, actually – a proper break, a real change. India maybe, why not?'

'India?' said Anne-Lise. 'Good idea.

'I hope you'll be able to get yourself organized, for once,' she added.

We ordered ravioli with cream and basil. I asked for a jug of water and Anne-Lise a half-carafe of wine. If she doesn't watch out, she'll end up an alcoholic. Every time I see her she's got a drink in her hand.

We chatted. That's to say, she drove me up the wall by totting up her lovers. I don't think I'm a prude, but I'm still surprised by some women's lack of discretion. Eric, Pierre, the other Eric and Vincent: I came close to knowing every-thing about these Prince Charmings, right down to the size of their little tools. Which I always find out about in the end, anyway. It's not that I'm turning my nose up, but hon-estly, sometimes it's embarrassing.

'Are you sure I'm not boring you?' Anne-Lise asked, dis-lodging a bit of ravioli from between her large incisors with a fingernail.

'Not at all, far from it.'

I listened patiently. Everything comes to an end, even Anne-Lise's list of lovers. Still, her habit of telling you about her every little entanglement seems incredible. As if that's all that matters in life – sex.

'You know Jean-Marc?' she asked me eventually, straight out, as if she'd just spotted him coming into the Grand Café.

I looked up, blushing, and mumbled, 'No, not really. I mean, yes, I think I may have met him in the office. He's a photographer, isn't he?'

Anne-Lise didn't notice my embarrassment. You might suspect her of being hard-hearted, but I think that she simply doesn't open her eyes wide enough to see the whole range of human emotions. Obviously I knew Jean-Marc. I even knew him well. He had come to my office on a number of occasions so I could sign expense forms or order plane tickets for him. And I'd dreamed about him for days on end. I should have guessed that the mere fact of seeing me sitting behind my files would drive him straight into Anne-Lise's bed.

'He's not just a photographer, he's also an exceptional lover,' said Anne-Lise, smirking.

There are certain feelings that are difficult to get used to. Disappointment, for example.

'How long have you been seeing him?' I asked, in a strangled voice.

'Oh, about a week,' Anne-Lise conceded, after pretending to search her memory. 'But I don't know if it's going to last.'

I didn't say anything. I stirred my coffee morosely and watched the sugar dissolving in the bitter, black whirlpool.

That was the stage I'd reached when Anne-Lise continued, her little eyes boring into the middle of my forehead. 'Have you come across haikus?'

'Hi what?'

'Haikus is what,' she said maliciously. 'Haikus. From Japan.'

Even after searching through the objects of my daydreams, I still couldn't remember any Japanese man called 'Haikus'. I shook my head.

'It's something Jean-Marc introduced me to,' Anne-Lise added, hurriedly. 'A sort of little poem, really deep.'

'Oh, right,' I said. 'Why did Jean-Marc introduce you to them? Is he Japanese as well?'

'No,' smiled Anne-Lise, slightly condescendingly. 'He's just come back from a story in Japan. Here, listen to this.'

She started to wriggle about on her chair, trying with difficulty to extract a scrap of paper from her back pocket. I could never understand how she managed to wear jeans that tight without exploding. And I daren't think about the state of her bum when she takes them off. Creased, probably.

'Here we are, listen to this,' she repeated, finally brandishing a little piece of folded paper at me. 'I copied one out at his flat this morning.'

I crooked my head to one side, praying she wouldn't read it out too loudly. Pointless, obviously. At the top of her voice, she announced:

> *The willow gazes*
> *At the heron's reflection*
> *Rippling upside down.*

A great blank silence enveloped the surrounding tables. Anne-Lise lifted her head and stared fixedly at me. For some time. All around, heads turned towards us, awaiting my verdict.

'Well, yes,' I finally admitted. 'That's poetry.'

Anne-Lise looked round, as if calling our neighbours to witness her grace and my foolishness. But wisely they'd already looked away, probably returning to more mundane conversations.

'*Poetry?*' she whispered. 'Really, darling, it's much more than just poetry. It's a whole philosophy.'

As if exhausted by such philistinism, she folded up the crumpled rag and embedded it in her pocket, snug against her behind.

'I read them every day,' she added, finally. 'And I can tell you that it's given me a completely different attitude to life. Really, this haiku thing has given my life a whole new dimension.'

I'm an open-minded kind of person. I've never been averse to adopting other people's good ideas. I'd even go so far as to say that I'm naturally curious. So I plied Anne-Lise with questions. When was the first haiku written? Who were the great haiku writers? Are there any anthologies in French? Naturally, Anne-Lise was incapable of answering even a quarter of my questions. And the few answers she did manage to come up with didn't seem that reliable. Given the speed with which she changes her interests, she can't slow herself down with too much background material.

At each of my questions, she knitted her brows with all the strength her little facial muscles could muster. Exactly as if it were an exercise to try and prevent wrinkles. For a moment I thought she was trying to get the attention of the guys at the next table. But she wasn't, they'd left.

Time had passed quickly, too quickly for my liking, as it did every time we had lunch together. We gulped down a second cup of coffee. Anne-Lise looked at her watch and pouted. Her whole face gathered round her mouth. With her fringe hanging down over her eyes, she looked like a pekinese, a huge, golden pekinese.

'Sweetie,' she said, 'I have to go now. Duty calls and it's a hard taskmaster. But why don't you come and have dinner on Friday? I've invited all my little gang.'

'Have you invited any men?' I asked, naively.

'Of course,' Anne-Lise answered, with her famous man-eating smile. 'Daniel will be there. You know Daniel adores you? He told me.'

I adore Daniel as well. But, for heaven's sake, not only is Daniel gay, he's also going out with somebody, and she knows that as well as I do. But still . . . It's always better to have dinner with other people than stay at home for a tête-à-tête with your cat. So naturally I accepted. I even said thank you.

We kissed each other goodbye in front of the café, then

she headed towards the Metro and I hurried off to get back to the office in time. We had barely gone our separate ways before that little word started roaming around endlessly in my head. Haiku.

The most earth-shattering events of our lives show up in the simplest ways. They arrive without fanfare – it's only afterwards, long afterwards, that we formally identify them. So, in that early afternoon when my new life had just begun, I walked innocently back to the office, my step even and my heart full of ignorance. But, in the tortuous convolutions of my life, destiny had started on its great work.

Haiku, I was thinking. Three little propositions that are sufficient to join together totally disparate scraps of the universe. Snatches of phrases swirled in my head so that I grew completely absorbed. I didn't think about Anne-Lise, or Jean-Marc, or my fax machine, or my cat, or all the evenings that I'd inevitably have to fill the next week . . . I accumulated words randomly as I walked.

When I got back to the office, I flipped carelessly with one finger through the time-sheets of my various free-lancers. Then I spent a substantial amount of time drinking a cup of coffee and pointlessly filing papers that no one would ever ask me for. I felt, how can I put it, weighty and cheerful. Full and busy.

On the stroke of five, after a day in which I had achieved nothing particularly useful for Global Promotions, I stole a new notebook from the stationery cupboard. I opened it at the first page but that seemed very blank. I turned to the second page, which felt some-how more approachable. I chewed the end of my pencil and then wrote in one go:

A glassy canal
Gliding over the black silt
The day takes its course

And there it was. I reread my little work. There was no
forced cheerfulness about it, but, such as it was, it
delighted me. In its simple, unshowy way, it addressed all
the anxieties of my life, in three little lines. I shut the notebook and looked at my watch. It was already nearly six
o'clock. I had stayed in that office so often outside my
regular hours, I had let it grow dark so frequently as I
sorted out problems that weren't mine, that I could allow
myself a little leeway. I decided to go home. Unless you
actively cultivate an unhealthy private life, you can't live
just for your work. You have to be able to say stop. So I put
my notebook in my bag and slipped discreetly out of
Global Promotions.

I went home on foot. The streets were full of hurrying
people. As I walked, I felt the same feeling of imperious
happiness that had gripped me all afternoon. I took streets
lined with different, unnecessary shops. Elegant passers-by
strutted along the aisles, haughty and expectant. I may be
only one-metre-sixty – just, if you count the soles of my
shoes – but I swear I didn't spoil the scene. I too strode
along with my head held high.

I returned home in triumph and kicked the cat, as it
wound itself round my feet, crying. I picked up the little
book next to the telephone, where, ordinarily, I noted down
my paltry engagements which I was in no danger of forgetting, anyway. For the second time that day, I composed a
little triplet:

Young girls are walking
Sharp-edged, discrete silhouettes
Between old buildings

The next day I rushed off to FNAC in my lunchbreak. Kilometres of aisles, millions of books, legions of customers, four staff. Or maybe five. I can't see how anyone would be able to find their way around unless they'd arranged the books on the shelves themselves. So I did what everybody does and asked. I took my place in the queue waiting in front of a counter. My turn inevitably came. A sharp-faced shop assistant pretended he had to bend down in order to be able to see me at the foot of his platform with its piles of catalogues.

'Yes?'

'I'm sorry, I'm looking for a book on Japan. On poetry,' I added, pitifully.

I don't know why the word 'poetry' found it so difficult to emerge from my terrified larynx. Anyway, the guy at the counter must have been too high up to be able to hear it.

'Tourism and Leisure, end of the aisle, next to the exit. Between Dieting and Gardening.'

'Thank you,' I whispered.

I didn't want to make a thing of it. That snobbish little way they have, bookshop assistants. I turned away, my heart on the verge of tears. And, believe it or not, I went to have a look at the Tourism section. For obedience's sake – because I'd been sent there.

That meant I was very close to the exit. I thought about leaving, because of all the things I didn't know, because I felt silly, because I was discouraged. Stooping, I got as far as the cash desks. But then I did a half-turn, and, with measured steps, hiding behind the turned-up collar of my jacket, I went back down the main aisle and ended up at the Literature section. I ambled along the panels of books, pretending to be a casual browser, vaguely curious, with time on my hands. I was about to give up when at last I found it. A series of annotated poetry collections were nestling in General Literature, sub-section Japan. Among them I glimpsed a copy of *The Book of Haiku*. I grabbed it and carried it off like a piece of precious treasure. As I headed towards the tills, I felt the book's weight in the hollow of my hand. It seemed alive, like a bird nesting in a hedge.

That evening I got into bed with my book and my cat. For the first time in weeks I didn't feel like kicking the cat, the heat thief, out of bed. We began reading together, then he fell asleep, pressed up against my side, snoring.

It's difficult to describe the happiness I felt that night. Let's just say that, as I lay there with my back propped against my pillow, I had the exquisite feeling that two immense lead doors were solemnly opening in front of me. What I'd suspected was now confirmed: this is what words can do, once they've been freed from the straitjacket of sentences. In this country, schools generally take it upon themselves to cure us of any love of language when we're five or six years old. But the Japanese have managed to keep the road that takes meaning to words clear. And they've made the most of it for almost a millennium. Intoxicated, I repeated a litany of haiku writers to myself: Basho, Buson, Issa, Shiki, Hekigodo, Kyoshi . . . Dear Anne-Lise. I fell asleep on the book.

We needn't talk about the excitement I felt for two whole

days. Balboa discovering the Pacific, Cabral landing in Brazil: there's no shortage of metaphors for the incredible joy I felt.

It was without enthusiasm, but with a strange sense of duty, therefore, that I went to the dinner party Anne-Lise had so generously invited me to. I arrived late, planning to melt discreetly into a crowd that would by that stage already be drunk. I had guessed right. They were all there, tipsy, and Anne-Lise, brazenly perched on Jean-Marc's thigh, was holding forth to her advertising friends.

Squashed together buttock to buttock, facing the low coffee table, Daniel and his boyfriend Darian were the only men not wearing jackets. Everyone was talking loudly and the babble hung like a canopy over the thick clouds of cigarette smoke. The guests nodded a greeting at me as I walked in. Daniel was the only person who smiled and I made my way through the gathering to squeeze in next to him. There was no room on the sofa, so I sat on the carpet at his feet.

'How are you, sweetheart?' he said, bending down towards me. Then, without waiting for an answer, he whispered in my ear, 'God, watch it. They're even more excruciatingly boring than usual.'

He meant Anne-Lise's friends. I glanced round the room. I'd already come across most of the assembled guests. Young, smug-looking men and young heavily-made-up women who were acting as though they'd been paid to bray with laughter round a bowl of peanuts. Interrupting each other constantly, repeating the same expressions endlessly, exclaiming in feigned suprise, they were spinning out a few meaningless anecdotes ad infinitum. Occasionally the incessant racket stopped in an awkward silence, which Anne-Lise would break with a shrill laugh or a cry of 'You'll never guess who . . .', tossed out rather desperately to her circle of friends.

I should never have accepted this invitation. Now I was going to be bored to death for an infinity which could have been spent reading quietly at home, lying next to my cat.

I couldn't even rely on Daniel to salvage the evening. We'd found ourselves sitting next to each other at so many dinner parties that we didn't have much left to say. We kept our confessions for the rare occasions when we were alone together. But liking one another in private isn't necessarily sufficient to get the conversational ball rolling at a trendy dinner party.

Daniel, who had one hand on Darian's knee, at least had the comfort of company. Admittedly, Darian, who was smiling in silence, seemed profoundly bored. But he was usually like that. Darian barely spoke French. He must be used to being somewhere without expecting or hoping for anything more than Daniel's loving presence and his hand on his knee. I envied them, protected by their love and coupledom. Abandoned on our end of the sofa, we were drinking in silence when Anne-Lise tore herself away from the ricocheting conversation, realizing that not everyone had been introduced.

'Christiane!' she cried, 'Daniel! I don't think you know Martine or her friend Bruno.'

We had every reason not to know them. And, given the choice, we would have preferred things to remain that way. But we were forcibly introduced.

'Where do those two come from?' I asked Daniel, after we had swapped names to mutual indifference.

'I know the girl. Anne-Lise has told me about her. She's a sales assistant. I think her parents are Korean. When

Anne-Lise was looking for extras for the Laboratoire Garnier ad, she called them. And, believe it or not, they agreed to do it. I don't know about him. I bet he's an officer in the sales battalion. He probably plays tennis and listens to Barry White. At any rate I'd be very surprised if he sold chips on the beach in a sarong, or played the trumpet at night in bars.'

There we were, whispering bitchily to each other, when we had to go to the table. The evening was a disaster, with one redeeming feature – it was passing. We could rely on the fact that, eventually, it would end, and everyone would go home. All we had to do was wait.

I plonked myself down at the end of the table next to Daniel, who'd sat down firmly next to Darian and put his hand back on his knee. God, that enviable capacity gays have for togetherness, even when they're alone. And the agony of heterosexuality and the inescapable solitariness, even when you're with someone.

Anne-Lise had excelled herself. From the inevitable tomato and mozzarella salad to the no-less-conventional generous bowl of pasta, every prerequisite of a fun, modern social gathering was catered for. The conversation turned to sports, where they were played and the equipment used. Tennis, squash and golf, to name but three. Lord have mercy. I was silent. I sat stolidly at my end of the table, a drab person with no personality. I was so aware of my own non-existence that I didn't even care about it any more. I was sure no one could see me, no one would remember me.

I took the opportunity to have a good stare at the men sitting round the table. Considered en masse, they looked tall and stupid. Raised on cereals, tanned on Breton beaches, you could make out, under their everyday weariness, a sort of rubbery, bourgeois resilience. At the end of every day each of them would have a five-o'clock shadow, a hoarse voice and a little sports car nonchalantly parked outside. It must be a comfortable feeling to have one of them at home for the evenings and weekends. It must be nice watching him tend his arsenal: his rackets and clubs, his car keys and well-cut jackets. Nice hearing him describe the brute strength needed to master the hostile soap, tyre, or yoghurt market. Nice, finally, to feel the weight of his big stupid body lying on your own – nice to touch, in a marital torpor, his grainy, familiar skin.

Which one, I wondered. Because when it actually came to making a choice, I kept being put off by a heavy chin, a fleshy neck, a throaty voice. I was pondering this question quietly, hidden behind my impenetrable gaze, when the conversation branched off into gastronomy and Anne-Lise brought a huge slab of decomposing brie to the table.

With hindsight, I can only put the little drama that ensued down to the brie and the wine. Jean-Marc was lavishly uncorking some more bottles of Bordeaux when Anne-Lise briskly changed the subject so that the conversation once more focused on her, the shining light.

'Who here,' she demanded point-blank, 'knows about haikus?'

At her side, Jean-Marc smiled self-deprecatingly. I kept quiet. My throat tightened with apprehension.

'I do!' piped up the minuscule Martine, who until then had been hiding in the shadow cast by big Bruno, restricting herself to fluttering her eyelashes at regular intervals. 'I do. They're little Chinese poems.'

'*Japanese!*' yelled Anne-Lise. 'Japanese!'

'Oh yes, Japanese,' whispered Martine, sinking her delicate face into her tiny shoulders.

> *The willow gazes*

Anne-Lise trumpeted,

> *The willow gazes*
> *At the heron's reflection*
> *Rippling upside down.*

I wasn't particularly surprised, but I did feel mildly disappointed. So, Anne-Lise hadn't thought it necessary to extend her repertoire since our last meeting.

'The haiku is much more than a little poem,' she expounded in a voice thick with tannin. 'It's a whole philosophy.'

I must have drunk quite a lot myself. Because, disregarding the consequences, I bluntly interrupted her from my end of the table.

'No, not a philosophy,' I said loudly. 'It's a whole way of life.'

Turning to look at me, Anne-Lise glared.

'Philosophy, way of life, it's all the same,' she cried across the plates.

I was about to retaliate when, to my dismay, little Martine used the moment's silence to draw attention to herself again.

'Yes,' she whispered, looking grimly in my direction, 'I completely agree with Anne-Lise, completely. Because . . .'

The table had fallen silent, flabbergasted by the novelty

109

of the conversation and its sudden violence. Turning away from Anne-Lise for a moment, Jean-Marc gave Martine a soulful look.

'Yes?' he said, inviting her to continue, amid the reverent hush.

'Because it's Zen,' she announced, in the voice of a pre-pubescent ant. 'It's very Zen.'

This time the gathering turned towards her as one. She gazed back at them with a matching hypnotized look. It was as if every one of those cretins had taken themselves for Pinto and was discovering Japan in person. And Martine, under the men's gazes, had assumed an authentic indigenous aura. Utterly authentic. And to think she's Korean. May her ancestors forgive her, I feel embarrassed for their spirits.

'Haikus,' she resumed, with a wheedling smile, responding to the expectations of the table. 'Haikus,' she continued. Her voice tailed off into her socks.

That was all. It was over. She dipped her neck gracefully, like a moorhen. For a few more minutes, the table kept up an expectant silence. Then, seeing it wasn't going to get anything else from the oracle except a panic-stricken smile half-hidden by her hair, it gave up.

'Fascinating,' murmured Jean-Marc. 'What was your name again?'

'Martine,' she whispered into the ashtray.

The racket started up again. I kept quiet, staring at my greasy plate. I had so much hatred inside me that I couldn't move – I was afraid it would overflow.

Cutting the brie into large wedges, Anne-Lise pretended to ignore me. I threw furtive bad-tempered looks at her. Then the doorbell rang.

'At last,' said Anne-Lise, 'Oliver . . .'

She rose awkwardly from the table and went to open the door, teetering on her endless legs. When she came back, she was dragging a man behind her who for once really was a contrast to her group of sporty, foodie friends. For a start, he was short. Secondly, he wasn't wearing a jacket. And finally, above all – he wasn't white. His skin wasn't white. That was the clincher. Because, after all, you don't find many non-white friends in our circles. Once again, silence fell on the dumbfounded group. Bravo, Anne-Lise. If she'd wanted to entertain her friends this evening, she'd certainly managed it.

'Typical Anne-Lise, always following the latest trends,' remarked Bruno, perhaps meaning the haikus but nevertheless making an unambiguous comment on the new arrival.

'Good evening,' said Oliver, unoffended by our dubious looks.

Obviously he was used to being in the minority.

'Don't get up. I'll grab a chair and sit at the end of the table. I've just come for coffee.'

'This is Oliver, everybody,' declared Anne-Lise triumphantly, running a hand through her impeccable blonde bob.

Then she turned to me.

'I met Oliver on the Sabena account,' she said curtly. 'He also works for Global Promotions from time to time. You're sort of colleagues. You have the same boss . . .'

Disaster. She'd invited him for me. At least that's what she was going to make out now. But what did she want me to do with him, this dark figure blown in by the night? I tried to defend myself, in desperate bad faith.

111

'That doesn't mean anything. We probably don't work in the same department. Or on the same floor. And I don't know all the freelancers.'

It was futile. Oliver was busy squeezing a chair in between Daniel's and mine. He sat down and smiled at me affably. He had a round face, fine, regular features and skin the colour of cloves. Without a shadow of a doubt, his roots reached back to the Indian subcontinent.

'Pleasure,' I conceded finally, once he'd sat down, but I refrained from giving him my hand.

He smiled again, inclining his head.

'I'm a translator. I've done work for you quite a few times. Maybe we've met?'

'Oh no. No, definitely not. I don't know everybody at Global. In fact, I'm quite cut off in my office.'

Anne-Lise was watching me warily across the table.

'So now's your chance to get to know each other,' she cried as exchanges began to start up again here and there around the table.

'Hmm,' I said.

She was clearly trying to palm me off on the first immigrant she could find. Why did she have to meddle in my life? Why couldn't she keep an eye on her photographer instead, who was now capturing the exotic Martine's face in a very tight focus? Why?

A basket of mandarins and lychees replaced the brie. I remained ferociously silent, deliberately ignoring my subcontinental neighbour, who, elbows on the table, was pretending to listen to the desultory conversation which somehow was still continuing. Daniel and Darian, enclosed in their affectionate bubble, whispered to each other, laughing. Once more I could hear Anne-Lise's

112

voice rising distinctly above the meal, and I champed at the bit.

'Oh no,' she yelped. 'Nothing like French poetry . . . It's much less, how can I put it . . . much less *elaborate*. We have very different sensibilities, you know? I mean, I'm not saying we're more civilized, or anything, but there's just no way you can compare Japan and Europe.'

She was going on shamelessly and she had gone too far. She deserved a thrashing. Furious, I banged my fist on the table.

'You're talking complete rubbish,' I shouted, to drown out the sound of her voice. 'Not only do you know nothing about it, but what you're saying is appalling crap. If you just thought for a second you'd see that it's perfectly possible to compare Apollinaire and Soseki, just for starters.'

'Steady, Christiane,' Jean-Marc interrupted, thumping his lap. 'You're not going to make a scene about some bunch of foreign writers who've been dead for bloody ages, are you? I mean, none of us even knows who these guys are. It's not worth it.'

'Shut up, you idiot,' I retorted. 'Of course it's worth it. I tell you, I'd rather have an argument about someone like Basho who's been dead for four centuries than about a moron like you. As for you, Anne-Lise, listen to this and then compare,

> *Copper-coloured sky*
> *No glimmer of light*
> *The moon seems to die*
> *And return to life.*

'So?' said Anne-Lise, stunned, as Jean-Marc ostentatiously nodded off, slumping into the lychees.

'So, that, believe it or not, is Verlaine.'

'So, what about Verlaine?'

'Oh, nothing,' I replied, discouraged. 'It was a comparison. But there's no point. You just don't get it.'

I fell silent, exhausted. She must have sensed the contempt beneath my weariness, though, because she suddenly flew off the handle.

'Stop getting so worked up!' she yelled. 'You're spoiling my whole dinner party.'

Then she called upon the table as a witness. 'Seeing as she's such an expert on the matter, Christiane is now going to recite us a genuine French haiku. Go on, Christiane, off you go. Share a little of your vast knowledge with us, if you don't mind.'

I didn't mind. I stood up, surveyed the table and said,

> *You stupid bastards*
> *You can go to fucking hell*
> *I'm going home now.'*

'Goodbye,' I added as I left the table.

'Goodbye,' chorused Daniel and Darian, who were the only ones laughing.

'Goodbye,' said the short dark man, looking up at me with interest.

The others watched me leave in silence. I slammed the door as hard as I could behind me.

The next day I was woken up by the telephone.

'Hello? Hello?' rasped Anne-Lise's voice.

'Oh shit,' I said to my cat and almost hung up. But she didn't give me a chance. She was on the offensive.

'Have you gone completely mad? What on earth got into you? Why did you get so angry? Jean-Marc thinks you need help. And Martine thought you were horrible.'

'Great,' I said. 'Who's Martine again?'

'The Chinese woman who was there yesterday.'

'Oh, do make a bit of an effort, Anne-Lise, she's Korean.'

'Same difference. You do realize you ruined my party, don't you? Do you have any idea how stupid you made me look?'

Suffocating under the landslide of recriminations, I didn't answer.

'Oliver left without saying a word about you. But you can bet your life you won't be seeing him again. That's the last time I invite someone for you. The last time. Because I did, I invited him specially for you, you know,' she insisted, bitterly.

'Oh well, if he was intended for me, then that must mean he likes boys, mustn't it?' I retorted. 'Phew, that's a weight off my mind. There I was, all night, stupidly worrying that I might have missed the one straight bloke left in Paris who you haven't bedded.'

'Me? Bedded? A black guy?' squawked Anne-Lise.

I slammed the phone down. God, she annoyed me.

As all this might imply, I stopped seeing Anne-Lise for quite a while after that. If it left me a little more lonely, I didn't notice. One evening I took down all the photos of friends I'd stuck up and gazed with pleasure at the white patch they left behind on the sun-faded wall. I stuffed them into a folder then filed it away with the year's payslips.

I left large white sheets of paper lying around the flat and wrote bitter little triplets on them. I'd laugh maliciously whenever I came across one.

> *The tongue flickers out*
> *The frog's great mouth opens wide*
> *And swallows the flies*

for example.

At Global I worked half-heartedly. I was gratified to see that, since our brief literary discussion, Jean-Marc had stopped coming into my office. Terrified, probably.

Then, a fortnight after the disastrous dinner party, I received an unexpected fax. In the middle of the page, a small, neat hand had written:

> *Suddenly I'm scared*
> *Something's happening. Moon*
> *through*
> *The mosquito net.* (Haku-un)

And below: 'I'm translating a sales brochure for Global at the moment. Will you have coffee with me tomorrow lunchtime? Fax me back. Oliver (the late arrival at your friend Anne-Lise's dinner party).'

I searched my desk furiously, sending clouds of dust and pages from my desk pad flying into the air. Finally I found what I was looking for. This, the answer, I sent back straight away:

> *The whole world is asleep*
> *Nothing at all left between*
> *The full moon and me* (Seifujo)

I can't tomorrow. What about the day after tomorrow, at

the Fountain Café by the office? If that's OK, no need to answer. Christiane.

We met up at the Fountain, shy and eager.

'I also admire Basho a lot,' said Oliver.

Need I go on? Oliver was, like me, a lonely heterosexual. He had dual nationality, French and English, an Indian family in Delhi, a PhD in Japanese and a Masters in Russian. He worked as a translator and wrote crude and lascivious pieces for a literary journal printed in Switzerland. We went to The Hague for the weekend to see the Mauritshuis. I invited him to dinner at my flat with Daniel and Darian. We planned on spending our next holidays together, with his family. Finally, on a Sunday, he moved his few pieces of furniture and countless books into my little flat. My cat ran away and never came back.

One morning I wrote on the back of an envelope:

> *A dark-haired man sits*
> *Smiling in my kitchen. He*
> *Lights a cigarette.*

Oliver was still asleep. I left the envelope on my pillow and went to work. In the evening, when I got home, I found a sheet of writing paper on the kitchen table which said,

> *My road stretches out*
> *A glittering ribbon. You*
> *Walk benevolent.*

'Do you want to marry me?' I asked him that evening as we ate supper facing each other across the kitchen table.

He stood up and came round to my side of the table. He lifted the hair off my ear and whispered,

'Sutejo writes,

> *The skin of women*
> *The skin they hide from the light*
> *How hot it is.*'

That's how we decided to get married. Three weeks later, Oliver was hired by an international organization. Appointed project leader, he had to find somewhere to live in Kyoto for two years. I took our furniture to a second-hand shop and bought two large trunks. I sent my resignation by registered post to Global Promotions. I bought our plane tickets. While we were waiting to leave, I stuck them on the wall. Then I picked up the telephone.

'Anne-Lise? It's Christiane.'

'Christiane?' answered the sugary voice. 'It's been ages! What's new, sweetheart?'

'What about you, dear, what's the Latest News in your eventful life?'

'Oh, you know . . .' sighed Anne-Lise, 'I'm really thinking about resigning. I'm sick of working twelve hours a day for an absolute pittance. If you ever hear of an assistant's job, could you think of me? That would be so sweet. I really want my life to change.'

'Of course,' I said, 'I'll have a think. How's Jean-Marc?'

'That bastard Jean-Marc, you mean. Guess what happened?'

'How am I supposed to guess? Tell me.'

'Well, he left. He left me to be with Martine. Can you believe it? Do you remember Martine? That little Japanese girl I was stupid enough to introduce him to on that legendary evening when you made such a fool of yourself?'

'I remember her very well. Still, I always thought Jean-Marc was a wanker,' I added, indulgently. 'I'm sure you can do better than him.'

'Yes, I'm sure. At the moment I'm going out with Bruno – you know? The tall silent guy who was with Martine back then. I'm not saying that it's forever between us – he's kind of glum, really. But anyway, we play squash, he lends me his car . . .'

'Well, that's something,' I said.

I looked at my watch. 'Right, Anne-Lise, I have something to tell you. You remember I told you I was thinking about taking a big trip one day when we were having lunch in the Grand Café? Well, I'm leaving in a week.'

'Where are you going?' Anne-Lise squawked, suddenly agog. 'Belgium?'

'No, Japan.'

'Japan?' Anne-Lise choked. 'You're going to Japan on your own?'

'No, I'm going with my husband. I'll call you when I get back,' I said hurriedly, without mentioning the distant nature of my return. 'Bye, Anne-Lise. Big kiss, see you soon.'

I hung up firmly. As I did so, I could still hear the shrill thread of a voice coming from the receiver, repeating tinnily, 'Your husband? Your husband? Your husband?'

I didn't have the urge – or the cruelty – to prolong this insignificant conversation. I called Daniel to give him my new address.

'If you hear of a sales assistant job, think of Anne-Lise,' I told him. 'She's looking.'

'You never know,' said Daniel.

I thought I heard him smiling on the other end of the phone.

7

THE KIWI-SELLER

YOU ONLY escape from loneliness in fits and starts. And friendship is responsible for many fits and starts. I love friendship. It's like the gulp of air torturers allow their victims before they push their heads back underwater. I don't have a problem with the taste of that breath. What I can't stand is the rest of the time, you're suffocating.

Mind you, friendship isn't the only thing that can pull our heads up out of the bath for a moment. There's also drink. And, above all, there's love. All of these things can give us the exhilarating feeling that we've escaped drowning. For a minute. People call this feeling happiness, and I do too. With reservations.

Hélène is a very good friend of mine. One of those friends you don't see too often because they have the good taste to let you live your own life. Every now and then we have lunch together. I pick her up from work. I walk up the street, go into her office building, and take the lift to her floor. She's there sitting behind her computer, waiting for me. Standing in front of her desk, I wait while she backs up her work, then we go and have lunch. Which is what we were doing, sitting opposite each other and discussing the random minutiae of our lives, when suddenly she interrupted me, her eyes staring.

'You *didn't*! You *can't have* slept with that beach blondie, that *kiwi-seller*? No, really, not with him?'

I hunched my shoulders and sank my chin into my collarbone. I twizzled my little finger vaguely in my glass of beer.

'I'm sorry,' I said, 'but I think I did.'

Hélène shook her head.

'I don't *believe* it,' she said. She spoke in little more than a whisper but – as she nodded, in a slight gesture of compassion – her voice struck me like a missile. Shame is an unpleasant sensation. Especially the resigned shame that you can sense someone feeling on your behalf. With that sort of shame, it's as if the whole universe is averting its eyes. It's better to suffer a thousand painful stabs of remorse, but do so alone, than to be slapped, just once, by the dismayed regret a friend feels for your sake.

Hélène looked at me, then looked away and inhaled nervously on her cigarette. Her disapproval hovered pallidly over me.

'*Anyone else*,' she repeated, 'even *Bruce Forsyth*, stark-naked, up against the fridge. But not him, not the kiwi-seller. I don't believe it.'

What was I supposed to say to that? I squeezed my legs together.

'Only once!' I burst out. 'It was only once, I swear!'

It was true. But that didn't excuse anything. When it comes to sex, once can be as bad as a thousand times. In fact sometimes a one-off is even worse than repetition. For women, sheer perseverance can end up being an extenuating circumstance, or even become a valid objective in itself. But a temporary aberration is sordid. Curiously enough, with men it's the other way round. See for yourself. Swap the terms of the proposition, and put 'men' where I wrote 'women'. Well?

'Hang on, I'm trying to remember,' said Hélène. 'It's not that guy who was so desperate to see us again after Emma's party, in February? That nervy little man with a ridiculous Southern accent?'

'Yes,' I conceded. 'It's that guy. But he has never sold a kiwi in his life.'

'Are you sure?'

'Certain.'

'Oh, well, I must be getting him mixed up with his brother,' remarked Hélène.

'You should be ashamed of yourself,' I said. 'That's making the way someone looks into a crime.'

'Not really. Look at it as more of a pre-trial investigation. This guy is facing a number of charges which if you add them up amount to an open and shut case. Firstly, he's got a Bordeaux accent. That in itself is pretty conclusive. Then he's got the sort of tan you only get if you spend all your time walking up and down the beach, half-naked, shouting, "Kiwis! Come and get your kiwis!" And last but not least, he's on the pull. Listen to those words carefully, roll them round on your tongue: He's On The Pull. Do you get it now? No one sleeps with a guy who's on the pull.'

'Alright,' I granted. 'Maybe they don't. Except me, that is. And you too, perhaps. Because you obviously know the whole story already. Not that I'm judging you. Everyone's gone out with a kiwi-seller at least once in their life, including you. Or am I mistaken?'

'Maybe just once . . . a barman, in a club,' Hélène said dreamily. 'But no, that doesn't count. Tell me what happened.'

'Do you remember the party?'

'Not really,' Hélène said.

'Well, the kiwi-seller followed me around all evening even though I didn't look at him once. When it was time to go and he was asking me for the tenth time how he could get in touch with me, I snapped, "Work it out for yourself." And bingo, he disappeared.'

'Far be it from me to criticize,' Hélène said emphatically. 'But, as far as I'm concerned, that amounts to a blatant invitation. So?'

'So – by this time it was morning and I went home by myself. My fiancé had got completely drunk and left without saying goodbye, after trying to hit on Emma. No big deal. It's a classic, isn't it? It's the one that goes, "The time he tried to get off with your best friend." Not that I blame anyone for these minor sickening aspects of life. Everyone has their reasons, and we're living in cruel times. But still, the fact remains that in the light of day I went home on my own.

'Days passed, bringing with them all the problems that seem to spring up wherever I go, like stones in poor people's fields. March comes around. One evening I get home and the answerphone is blinking. I press *Play* and hear a voice I don't recognize. Surprised, I sit down on the floor. It's a good thing I do because there's a whole hour of chatting about this and that and suggesting we should meet. The entire tape. He'd tracked me down and then used up my entire tape.'

'Idiot,' said Hélène.

'I don't know. I have to say I thought it was nice of him to have gone to all that trouble. So when he rang back that evening, I picked up. I felt quite happy to see this man who had made such an effort to find me again. I was a bit nervous as well, though. You don't just *hang out* with people from totally different worlds. Maybe I was ashamed of my curiosity, my easiness.'

'Nothing's going to come of this,' I told him on the phone.

'That's lucky. I don't want anything to,' he replied. 'I just want to see you. Say a place, anywhere, a day, any day, and a time, and I'll hang up.'

I was taken by surprise, caught between my ambivalence and his desire to get organized. So I said, 'Thursday, seven-thirty, at the Café Français.'

He hung up. As a safeguard, I immediately arranged to meet someone for dinner at eight-thirty.

Thursday comes, it's seven-thirty-five, and I'm running towards the Café Français, dishevelled, with a headache, moaning to myself, 'Why did I agree to meet him? Why do I always put myself in such impossible situations?'

I saw him before I even pushed open the door. He was sitting stupidly by the window, not even reading a newspaper, just waiting and watching the passers-by.

'I haven't got any space in my life,' I told him, sitting down next to him without taking off my jacket.

'I don't want any space,' he said.

'Oh, come on, don't be stupid. We both know why you're here.'

'Oh. Why's that, then?'

He was playing the innocent. Where did he learn to do that? In Bordeaux? I decided to put my foot down.

'So we'll end up in bed together, of course. I can tell you right now that it's not going to happen.'

'If you know that already, then why did you come?'

Honestly, what an outrageous question. It left me speechless – and wondering, incidentally, why *had* I come? I was obviously there, so I had to give him an answer. I racked my brains, trying to work out the truth. Which was stupid, of course: although people like to think of the truth as something practical, solid and indivisible, in fact it's elusive, fragmentary and useless.

'Out of curiosity, maybe,' I said eventually, 'or perhaps just for fun, playing around, you know.'

It was the most sincere thing I could think of at that precise moment. I soon regretted saying it, though.

'Playing around?' he echoed. 'Brilliant! I love games. Let's both play, and we'll see who wins . . .'

He breaks into a huge grin. This guy has at least fifty-two teeth. He's pleased. He's hit on an idea, and he's not about to let go of it in a hurry. What am I doing sitting next to this imbecile?

The more he annoys me, the more I look at him. I take in his appearance, involuntarily appraising and calculating. I examine his particulars. He's short and thin. He's chosen, then ironed, his outfit – what is that ridiculous waistcoat? When his crash helmet slips off the next-door table and he dives and catches it in mid-air, I observe how agile he is, and note his tanned neck.

'So, what do you do with your life?' he continues once he's upright again. As if we're destined to get to know each other.

'Oh, my life,' I say, 'it's all just work and love affairs.'

I admit this was a despicable piece of flirting. But, after all, you could also see it as an – admittedly abrupt – précis of all our lives. And in fact I was only trying to reassure him that his tenacity was legitimate: there are good reasons for desiring – as there are for regretting – a woman who makes a profession of her freedom. I was just returning the favour, embodying for the occasion the simple, smiling figure of the strumpet.

'Work and love affairs . . .'

He quivers with pleasure and gazes at me longingly. Yes, he has got an accent. I suspect he's waiting for another witticism. I look at my watch.

'Right, it's time I was off,' I say without looking at him, my face a blank mask like a cobra's, 'I've got a dinner to go to and I'm already late.'

I give him a sidelong look. All of a sudden, he seems unhappy. His smile withers and there's only his face, the fine features of his face. Some men who ordinarily look old – full of mournfulness and regret – can suddenly look just as they did as children. It's a celebrated truth known to women.

'I thought we were going to have dinner,' he says, frowning.

'That wasn't what we agreed.'

I get to my feet, pay for the coffees and pick up my bag. 'Bye, then,' I say.

He stays where he is, in his ironed polo shirt, sitting in his chair disappointedly and watching me leave. Then he changes his mind, jumps up and grabs his helmet.

'Hang on, I'll drop you off,' he says, following me, sticking to my back like a jellyfish.

We're the same height. He holds the door open for me. I sweep through in front of him, the Queen of Sheba, vaguely inclining my head with a sort of gracious bobbing motion I associate with wading birds. On the pavement, I turn to face him in order to sound the parting knell. But he ignores my farewell look.

'Come on, I'll give you a lift on my scooter,' he offers, before I have time to open my mouth. And he points to some kind of moped, parked in the middle of a row of black and red motorbikes, covered in stencils. A horrendous pattern of blue and green blobs. Not a scooter so much as a *surfboard.*

'Oh no. How could you?' sighed Hélène. 'A *kiwi-coloured scooter . . .*'

'Exactly. I'm suddenly scared sick that someone might see me. I look around to check that no one I know is hanging about. "No thanks," I say hurriedly. "I've got to go."

'"Hang on," he says, catching me by the sleeve. He takes a scrap of paper out of his pocket. "Give me a pen."

'I search through my backpack, and pass him an expiring biro. Resting the paper on his raised knee, he writes down his phone number. Then he gives me back the pen and quickly opens my bag and stuffs the piece of paper into it.

'"All you've got to do if you want to call me, one day, is leave this lying around in the bottom of your bag. It's valid for three months. After that you'll probably clean out your bag, or else it'll have fallen to bits."

'"Thanks," I say. "Bye." And then I turn away, before I have to watch him climb on to his painted scooter, before anyone sees me in his oppressive company. End of Part One.'

'You should never have met up with him,' Hélène observed.

'Maybe not, but I don't know how to go about standing someone up,' I pointed out. 'We can't all be as cool-headed as you are. I just let myself get caught up in the chain of events.'

'No, the real problem is that you can't say *No*. Or maybe it's that you always want to say *Yes*.'

'Probably. Anyway, a month later, Part Two. It's the middle of April and I am the obliging victim of my own life. Under the pretext of repainting the upstairs room, an Algerian painter without a work permit has more or less moved in with me. He smokes hash all day and learns my videos off by heart. I've lent him a copy of the Koran. He comments on all my visitors, not that he's passing judgement on the quantity or quality of the men in my life, of course. I want to kill him and wall up his corpse in the cupboard upstairs.

'Jilali,' I say to him one day, as I clear away a bottle of red wine that's been left next to the video, 'doesn't the Koran say that drinking is forbidden?'

'The Koran's like the Gospels, you have to know how to read it,' he replies, handing me my address book which he's just sat on.

Friday. It's getting dark. I'm tired from work, and from spring which is just beginning to settle in the foliage on the avenue's trees. At night you can hear the birds panicking. They arouse a great, abandoned, feverish feeling which always comes over me at the end of the winter. It's nearly eight p.m. by the time I listen to the answering machine. Among the usual jumble of my everyday life, I hear two untimely pieces of news.

'Hi,' says the voice of my beloved fiancé, 'I'm calling from the airport. I'm going to a friend's wedding in Anvers and I'll be staying until the start of next week. I'll call when I get back.'

'Hi,' says the voice of my friendly lover, 'I'm going to Hyères with my parents. I'm not staying long. I'll be back Sunday morning. I'll call from the airport.'

Mr Six-of-One and Mr Half-A-Dozen-of-the-Other. I'm left on my own on the eve of creation. Time splits in two like a piece of rotten fruit. The moments pass silently, creeping along behind each other on tiptoe. That Friday evening is as broad as the Danube. I can't see the other bank. Filled with melancholy, I let the night seize hold of me. The flat seems too big and I wander along the passage, thoughts moving slowly through my mind. My bag is lying on the floor; I pick it up, search through it, take out the kiwi-seller's number and call him.

'Why him? Why not someone else? Why not me?' Hélène interrupted.

'Because it was late. Because I'd run aground on the shoals of time and was ashamed of my trawler soul. Because a friend is no use at a time like that – the best they can do is be a kind of warm poultice. Because I wanted to be on my own, so long as there was someone else there with me.'

'Bollocks,' Hélène observed.

'Exactly, complete bollocks. Anyway, I think to myself that there isn't much chance that he'll be at home, so late on a Friday night. Chance has already played such a big part in all this that I'm happy to shelter under it as if it were a huge umbrella. I dial the number.'

'And he answers.'

'Oh, yes. "Nice timing," he says, "I was just on my way out." But he's round in twenty minutes – scooters are pretty nippy, I guess, when you think about it. He rings the bell and I open the door. Neatly ironed clothes. Big smile. Round-eyed. One and the same. "Who is this guy?" I wonder, as I let him in.

'I offer him coffee but he'd rather have tea. Five minutes later I've put on some music and we're sitting on the carpet. At that stage of the evening he's quietly contemplating me with a knowing smile. Not making the slightest move. Just sitting there, patiently, his nose in his cup of tea, waiting for me to make conversation.'

'What a pain,' chuckled Hélène.

'What a strain, more like. I ask him about his job and his family. I don't even really hear his answers, I'm bored. I forget everything he says the minute he's said it. It's weird: I can't seem to summon up any interest in who he is, I just don't care. Meanwhile time is getting on.'

He has no idea of the effort I'm making. His velvety eyes study me from behind their lashes. He's overflowing with affection. He probably loves the sound of my voice. He trusts me, I think. He can't imagine that I could wish him the slightest harm. So he stares at me with an enthralled expression, his chin lifted so as not to miss a word I'm saying. I realize we could go on like this till next year.

'OK,' I say finally, infuriated. 'It's nearly one in the morning. It's pretty late. What are we going to do now?'

'Carry on playing, of course,' he says, rubbing his thighs in a manic way. 'We're right in the middle of the game and I'm wondering who's going to win.'

Give an idiot an idea and he'll boomerang it endlessly

back at your head. It's as dangerous as giving a hamster a wheel. They just can't stop pedalling.

'Who's going to win what?' I say curtly. 'There's nothing to win. Besides, I never play games. I loathe them. That was just an idle thought.'

He doesn't reply immediately. He looks upset as he runs his fingers through his frizzy Bordeaux hair. He looks like a toy that's been lost in a station. Or a little boy who's been slapped by mistake. Great. It's all my fault. This poor guy has got up in the middle of the night only to be given a hard time, all because of my seasonal nostalgia. And now I'm going to kick him and his abandoned expression out into the night, am I? I mull it over. In his face I see reflected the feeling of pointless freedom I have in my heart.

After all, it's off season. I decide that this is the night when people of the same height will stick together. I feel a surge of courage, altruism and loneliness. With my head bowed, I plunge deeper into the generous tunnel of pretence and half-lies I've been digging since the start of this business.

'Let's kiss and then you can go, alright?'

That's what I say. So he won't leave without a souvenir. So we won't part as cold as when we met. So I can taste the flavour of his brown skin. So I can see.

'Alright,' he says.

Straight away I go over, bend down and kiss him. I take his face in my hands and give him a proper kiss, deep and attentive. Surprised, he stays glued to the sofa. His mouth is soft, his lips well-defined, his body slim and familiar under his light clothes. It's a real kiss, believe me. Twenty years' training, three minutes' demonstration. But when I pull my face back and meet his unhappy eyes, I'm brought down to earth. He shakes his head.

'Oh, no,' he says, 'no, that's not OK at all.'

'What's not OK?' I ask, offended.

He thinks. 'Well, it's not what I wanted.'

'Oh, really. What did you want?'

He is visibly lost for words. I watch his vocabulary struggle within the walls of his feelings.

'I'm sorry,' he says eventually, 'but I was thinking of something more like this.'

Now it's his turn to come over and, in the sweetest way possible, enfold me in his arms. He hugs me to him familiarly, as if we've known each other since school. His slender fingers run over my neck and my shoulders. The vague promise of sleep and the colours of childhood come into my head, like a warm memory of happiness. When my head slips into the hollow of his neck, he leans down further and his lips graze my mouth. He rocks us imperceptibly back and forth, lulling us in a scented, whispering embrace.

'That's more what I wanted,' he confirms when he steps back, his hands resting on my shoulders.

I sit down and look him in the face. He stares back at me, searching for some feeling behind my calm expression. But I just smile feebly. He puts his hand to his hair. I see the relief lift, slowly, like a veil, from his features.

'Perhaps I should be going now.' He stands up and picks up his helmet which is lying beside the sofa. 'It's one-thirty. You must be tired.'

I think he's trying something on. But he's not. With an incredible time-lag, he's finally realized that he's in my way. And accepted it. He's getting ready to go, in silence. Just when the wind's turning. Just when I've changed my mind.

This guy is definitely one of those people who gets the point alright – just at the wrong time.

'No,' I say, hanging my head, 'you should stay. It's very late.'

He turns. He hesitates – he's trying to work it out. In the end he trusts his intuition.

'OK, fine,' he says, quickly putting his helmet back down on the floor.

So there we were. We brushed our teeth, side by side, like a pair of pensioners. We got undressed, side by side, like a couple of worn-out ramblers. Then we got into bed, without saying much, like two monks.

I felt reassured, seeing him lying next to me. He had a lovely body, lovely skin, a lovely mouth, lovely eyes. I turned towards him and slipped into his arms as if it was the most natural thing in the world. We were both very pleased with each other.

'Mmm,' I remarked.

'Pink?' he asked, picking up his trousers from the foot of the bed and taking a little packet of condoms out of the pocket.

'Or green?' I said, stretching out a hand to get the packet lying in my desk drawer.

I thought of Sleeping Beauty's wedding dress and the two fairy godmothers making it change colour with a wave of their magic wands. I smiled to myself.

'Do you know any Walt Disney films?'

'Yes,' he answered, surprised. 'Why?'

'Because I adore them.'

He looked at me, appalled. 'Really? I think they're kind of stupid.'

I should have known. I took his face in my hands and looked at him lustfully to stop him saying any more. To stop him saying anything at all, in fact. He must have guessed – he laughed kindly.

After that we got on admirably. I kept remembering a summer night of twenty years earlier, which I'd spent on a beach in the experienced arms of a mechanic who loved Johnny Hallyday. I had forgotten that night as completely as I'd forgotten the boy's face. And there it came back to me, full of sand and darkness. I remembered the colour of the skirt I was wearing, dotted with little blue peacocks. I remembered the purring of the sea and the awkwardness of calling someone I was never going to see again by his first name.

'You think I'm stupid, don't you?' he asked, after we'd each rolled over to our side of the bed.

'No,' I said, partly lying and partly not really having an opinion, in that state of sweaty collapse which often passes for feeling.

'Why did you ask me to stay?' he insisted. 'I didn't want to cause you any more hassle. I was about to leave.'

'Because you made such a thing about it. Or because I felt like it. A bit of both, probably.'

'But why did you call me in the first place? You didn't want anything to do with me, last time.'

'No, but tonight I was on my own.'

'You could have called a friend, someone you know.'

'I didn't want to have to make the effort to be nice. Friends need attention. They're demanding. You can't just ask them to come round in the middle of the night.'

'Why? If they come, it's because they want to.'

'But that's not an excuse to use them. Besides, they're

135

tiring. From the moment they become friends, you've got to accept that they'll bore you with their feelings.'

'And my feelings don't count . . . You don't care in the slightest whether I'm happy or unhappy?'

'I haven't even thought about it. Without a shared past or future, we barely exist for each other. You're the one who's making such a thing about it. I mean, if you feel something now, it's your own fault.'

'But now is what I'm talking about. Don't you care at all about how I feel now?'

'A little.'

'Why?'

'Because I know you a little now. So it's best if we don't see each other again. It'll only lead to trouble.'

'Even if I swear not to be unhappy?'

'Yes, even then. Anyway, I wouldn't believe you.'

'It could just be casual between us.'

'No it couldn't. You're not casual any more. You're entitled to have feelings.'

'And you don't want to give me and my feelings a go?'

'No, because we're not in love.'

'What do you know?'

It was stupid. I laughed nervously. Then we fell asleep.

'How was it in the morning? Hard?' asked Hélène.

'He asked for hot chocolate.'

'Hot chocolate?'

'Yes. Does that surprise you?'

'Not at all. I was expecting hot chocolate. I was hoping for it. You can't have a Bordeaux surfie without hot choco-late. And then what?'

'Then he asked if he could look at some photos which

were lying around with the stuff cluttering up my desk. I was in my nice sunny bathroom, getting out of the shower and not really thinking, so I said sure.'

They were photos of the spring holiday I'd been on with my fiancé. When I went back into the bedroom, after I'd finished drying myself, he was still looking at them, those mementoes of walks and panoramas showing the two of us taking turns at smiling happily into the camera. He looked gravely up at me.

'You were lying,' he said, looking me in the eyes.

'When?'

'When you said you worked and had love affairs. You didn't tell me you were with someone.'

'So?'

'So, it's not right.'

'What's not right?' I asked suspiciously, pulling the towel up to my shoulders. He waved the photos under my nose.

'You were lying. "Love affairs" isn't true.'

'How do you know?' I said, taking the photos and tossing them back on to the jumble strewn over the desk.

'Because it's obvious from these photos,' he insisted. 'Don't tell me we're not going to see each other again because we're not in love. Tell me it's because you've got a man in your life.'

'I don't see what difference it makes.'

'Oh, come on, it makes all the difference. Can't you see any distinction between a woman who's already in love with a man and a woman who isn't in love with anybody yet? You can't pay that much attention. You're not very sensitive, are you?'

'Maybe not,' I said.

'I'm not criticizing you,' he continued, in a milder voice. 'But you should change the way you put things. When you talk about "games", or "lovers" or "feelings", you're just messing about with words. It's all pretty casual. No one knows where they stand any more.'

Without any drama, he'd just put my garrulous, sketchy life into perspective. Where, in what corner of himself, was he finding this understanding of me and my love affairs? Where was he getting this unexpected wisdom which was now tumbling down on me without my having asked for anything?

A few minutes later he was standing on the doorstep, wearing his jacket, with his helmet under his arm.

'Goodbye,' he said, hugging me warmly. 'I'm sorry you're not free. I would have carried on ringing you for a while.'

'That's the way it goes,' I said. 'Are you angry with me?'

'No,' he replied brusquely. 'There's something quite likeable about it.'

He was leaving. Maybe he could have stayed. He could have taught me how to tidy away photos rather than leaving them lying about on my desk. I could have showed him how to crumple his clothes. We wouldn't have talked much but we'd have slept well. He'd probably have lost his accent, in the long run. I would have been happy, and maybe he would have, too. At least for a fortnight.

I was silent. He scrutinized me, holding my gaze slightly too long. My wave of affection broke.

'You're not going to call me again, are you?' he said eventually.

'I don't think so.'

'Pity. Maybe we'll see each other around.'

'Maybe.'

Then he left. And that's the story.

'Have you seen him again?' said Hélène.

'No. He called one evening, a few weeks later. To finish it I told him that I was moving in with my fiancé. He sounded surprised. "Already?" he said. "This minute?"

'"Yes, this minute," I said, feeling uncomfortable. I didn't want to drag it out, so I hung up as soon as I could. That's all. Now you know how you sleep with a kiwi-seller.'

Hélène stubbed out her cigarette.

'It's a sad story,' she said.

'You think so?'

'Yes. Everything about it is sad: the Friday evening, the guy, the guy leaving. It all comes from having nothing to do. Or from being bored. Both of which states, mind you, I'm familiar with.'

'You don't think it's more like a tiny little love story?'

'Oh, please,' said Hélène, 'don't try and bung in feelings everywhere. You're amazed because you've discovered that everyone has a soul. But it's not that much of a great revelation. I could have told you that myself. Everyone has a soul. Even kiwi-sellers. There's no need to sleep with them to find that out.'

'Yes, but it's a really moving thing for me to realize that someone is alive. All you see is a shadow and then suddenly it's a person who catches hold of you, another living person. I feel I should celebrate that. It's as if I've been saved, as if I'm being given a second chance.'

'Pure paganism,' said Hélène. 'Watch out, people have been sectioned for less.'

'I think being too severe can do you harm,' I said.

'I don't think being too sentimental has much charm, either,' Hélène said.

I'd come to the end of my story. We were sitting in dismal silence when the waiter finally decided to come and take our order.

'Oh,' said Hélène, scrunching up the menu distractedly, 'I'm not very hungry.'

'Me neither,' I said. 'I'll just have a salad and some bread.'

'Me too,' said Hélène.

'Lost our joie de vivre, have we, ladies?' said the waiter.

'Our *what*?' barked Hélène, snapping her menu shut.

'Nothing – sorry, madam – I didn't mean anything,' the waiter mumbled, pocketing his order pad. He hurried off to the kitchen.

8

TAKING IT TO HEART

'SATURDAY AFTERNOON, for tea. Is that alright, if I come on Saturday afternoon?'

Granny hesitated for a second. 'I don't know if I'll be able to see you,' she said, sounding preoccupied.

'I'll bring Théo,' Bénédicte added.

'Speak up. I'm going deaf. I can't hear very well on the telephone these days.'

'*I'll bring Théo!*'

'Oh, well, in that case, if there's two of you,' Granny said, 'it won't be such a long drive.'

'Don't worry. Even if I drive carefully, it doesn't take more than two hours.'

'But it's still quite a journey. And don't expect anything wonderful now, will you? I'm not up to cooking anything elaborate any more.'

'That's fine,' Bénédicte interrupted. 'We're coming to see you, not for the food. OK, big kiss. See you on Saturday.'

On Saturday, Bénédicte got up at ten, drank a cup of coffee, had a shower and dressed in summer clothes. At ten-thirty, she left an avalanche of messages on her brother's answering machine. At eleven-thirty she rang his doorbell.

Puffy-eyed and half-asleep, Théo opened the door, a towelling dressing gown loosely wrapped round him.

'Hey,' he said, 'it's only eleven-thirty! You said you were coming at midday . . .'

'Are you trying to be funny? I've left ten messages this morning. Couldn't you even pick up?'

'I didn't hear anything,' he said, lowering his head and rubbing his mouth with the back of his hand.

She shook her head. 'It's alright, it doesn't matter. Go and have a shower, I'll make some coffee.'

She sat on his bed and drank another cup of coffee while she waited for him to get ready. He was singing in the shower. The flat smelt of coffee, soap and aftershave.

At one o'clock they shut the door of his studio flat. At five past they climbed into her Alfa.

'Can I drive?' asked Théo.

'No way,' answered Bénédicte. 'When are you going to pass your test?'

'Stop it. You sound like Mum.'

'Oh, really,' said Bénédicte. 'Fasten your seat belt.'

'Forget it,' Théo replied.

'Fine, we won't go then.'

Bénédicte put the keys on the dashboard and folded her arms.

'OK, OK, I'll put my seat belt on, but you are just like Mum.'

They left Paris by the Porte de Bagnolet, then turned off the *périphérique* and joined the traffic flowing along the

A1. Théo sank his chin on to his chest and closed his eyes, his mouth slightly open. He fell asleep, his chest lolling towards the windscreen, held up by his seat belt.

Bénédicte adjusted her seat so that she could stretch her legs and reach the pedals by moving only her toes. She turned down the car radio a little and sank deeper into her seat. She held the steering wheel with one hand, and rested the other on the gear stick.

They passed the buildings bordering the outskirts of Paris, then the banks of trees hiding the rows of suburban houses, then Roissy's tunnels, over which huge aeroplanes glided slowly. Roissy signalled the end of Paris, the start of Picardy, the first fields and woods, hillier countryside.

Bénédicte listened to Théo sleeping and reminisced vaguely about the thin, pale *tarte aux pommes* Granny used to bake them for tea. She'd make the pastry the day before with wheat flour. The sweet smell of apples used to blend with that of the furniture polish, filling the warm flat.

As they passed Roye, Théo opened his eyes and worked his mouth like a sick bird. He bent forward and picked up the bottle of mineral water rolling around at his feet, then he drank from it for a long time, making painful swallowing sounds.

'Are we there yet?' he called out to his sister, tossing the bottle on to the back seat.

'Any moment now,' Bénédicte replied. 'So, how do you feel? Pleased to be going back to the family's stamping grounds?'

'The family? What family?' retorted Théo. 'They've all moved, I don't know them any more. As for stamping

143

grounds, since the houses were sold, all I can think of is the graveyard. That's where most of them are now. Do you know who looks after the graves?'

Bénédicte thought for a moment.

'Granny, probably.'

'What? She's more than eighty.'

'So? Don't you know she's going to live till she's two hundred? She'll be looking after your grave too. Give me a cigarette.'

'Has it been a long time since you've seen her?' asked Théo in a muffled voice.

'No, I saw her last month.'

'Last month?'

'Yes. Why? Does that surprise you?'

'It makes me feel guilty. I haven't seen her for six months.'

'I know. You're a bastard.'

'True. But I'm making up for it now. Change lanes! Come on, change lanes! You're like a Sunday driver.'

'*North-East* rhymes with *deceased*,' Théo observed as they passed Lille-Lesquin airport.

'And with *yeast*,' Bénédicte said, '*priest* and *increased*. Light my cigarette for me, will you.'

Théo pushed in the cigarette lighter. He was thinking about the places in which they'd grown up, that had now disappeared. He was always hoping, by some sleight of memory, to see them again. But time had erased them – first quietly, insidiously, then with furious speed.

He felt that he had been brutally robbed of the map of his childhood, with its dark, stagnant-smelling lanes behind the houses and its tall furnaces rising like bell-towers above the narrow, cobbled, treeless streets. His time had, literally, been wasted.

'I loved its sadness,' he said. 'I swear, I used to love the rain hissing in the dark streets and the grass sprouting between the cobblestones. I loved it all, even the dregs, the deadened colours, the winter that lasted all summer, the houses built around their lukewarm kitchens. It's such a shame – there's nothing left to love now. All that's left is grotesque, deserted housing estates full of fake houses built out of fake bricks – no doubt in some misplaced attempt at local colour.'

'I don't like architects,' agreed Bénédicte.

'Christ, neither do I. Before I die, I'd like to beat the shit out of an architect as revenge. Any one will do – although I'd prefer a puny one, if possible.'

They had passed Lille. The motorway slip road now fed them directly from the bypass into their past, bringing them on to the broad boulevard leading from Lille to its sub-urbs. Bénédicte began, precise and ritual, 'When I worked for the *Nord-Éclair* . . .'

'. . . I used to cycle along this road twice a day – fourteen kilometres there and fourteen back,' finished Théo, who knew the refrain so well that he felt sorry not to have quoted it in full without having to be prompted. 'You must have nice legs,' he remarked.

'I have got nice legs,' said Bénédicte.

Then she fell silent. At thirty kilometres an hour she drove alongside the park where they'd got bored during summers, past the trees under which they used to arrange to meet their friends. She parked in front of the secondary school. Then she stayed motionless, both hands on the steering wheel, looking at the closed doors.

'There's no point coming back,' Théo said, breaking the silence. 'Personally, this little commemorative detour is the last of its kind I'm going to inflict on my long-suffering memory.'

'Does it upset you?' asked Bénédicte, turning to look at her brother's face.

'No, it makes me sick,' he said. 'I'd like to be someone else and not have anything to remember here. I'd like to be able not to care about you.'

Bénédicte slowly drove the remaining kilometres between them and the house they'd lived in for almost twenty years.

They sat down next to each other on the kerb. In the heavy, clammy heat, they gazed at the front of the house. Bénédicte had rolled the sleeves of her polo shirt up on to her shoulders. She distractedly raised a can of lager to her lips as she looked at the closed front door. Théo, his knees apart, his head bent, rolled a can of lemonade between his hands. The misted surface left a cold film on his palms.

The house had been sold when their parents went to live further south. There had been too much furniture for their new flat, so it had been partially dispersed.

Behind the house's tall, varnished wooden door ran a tiled passageway which ended in a broad staircase leading up three floors. A backstairs ran up to the attic.

The ground-floor passage led to a bright kitchen, which gave on to a small garden. Enclosed by brick walls covered in ivy and Virginia creeper, the garden was bisected by a paved path lined with earthenware pots of geraniums. The miniature beds changed colour all year round, as Busy Lizzies combined with anemones, or

TAKING IT TO HEART

chrysanthemums with asters. Plants proliferated at every level, flowering briefly and sending out their watery scents in succession – hydrangeas, roses, privet, wisteria, a lilac thrusting straight up to the sky, a syringa. The path led to three square metres of grass surrounded by periwinkles, and beyond that to a circular slate patio ringed with ferns.

At the end of the garden, against the wall, constantly cut back yet still enormous, an ash stretched out its heavy branches invitingly for children.

'If you ever moved house,' Théo had said to his mother one day as she sat sewing at the garden table, 'if you ever moved house, I think I'd have to kill you.'

She had put down her sewing and given him a long, mistrustful look, staring at his little face without compassion.

'Then you'd go to prison,' she'd remarked.

'I'd go to prison but I'd get to keep the house.'

He seemed to think that the exchange was over. But, wanting to instil less impetuous sentiments in her son, she'd insisted, 'A child doesn't kill his mother because she wants to move house. That just doesn't happen.'

Théo had been more swayed by her certainty than by her threat.

'Well, if you move,' he'd conceded, 'you'll be on your own. I'll stay here. I can get a dog.'

Throughout May, the garden bore flowers which decorated the little statue of the Virgin on the dresser.

'I don't want to be here any more,' Théo blurted out, getting up from the pavement. 'I'm scared someone will open the door of the house and come out as if it's their home. That would kill me.'

'You always exaggerate,' said Bénédicte. 'Get in the car, we're going to Granny's.'

Granny had lived with Grandfather for forty years in a large flat which she didn't much like and which had caused her a great deal of worry. Grandfather had died in the end, thereby liberating his son and daughter-in-law who wasted no time in moving. They assured Granny that they'd care about her just as consistently from a distance. She realized they had fled.

Granny viewed her son and daughter-in-law's departure as confirmation of her suspicions, and she felt unexpectedly relieved. She had always believed she was alone in the world; at last she could be so in peace. She found time to write to her friends, pray for her grandchildren, and succumb to lengthy bouts of paranoia, which tended to be followed by violent fits of depression. She thought about Grandfather often and sometimes talked out loud to him as she took faltering steps across large polished floors.

'My baby,' she'd say, 'you little rascal, I know you're there.'

Since she'd read Teilhard de Chardin, Granny's faith had been seasoned with a sort of improvised animism. She was an enthusiastic, if unpredictable, interpreter of religious texts.

Grandfather had turned his back imperceptibly on a disintegrating, collapsing world. The only outward sign of this, at first, was his vivacity. They had even regarded his fondness for puns and his passion for women as virtues that promised a sprightly retirement for this inflexible and secretive man. Then the witticisms grew more silly and he started to follow female passers-by, forgetting his way home, no doubt overcome with wonder at his capacity to make out their warm behinds under their thick coats. Lost in the town in which he'd spent his whole life, he'd wander the streets at night, unconcerned, a little figure in a grey hat and overcoat.

His replies to questions grew random and he'd repeat the same scraps of phrases tirelessly, an impish smile on his face, his eyes distraught. The disk had wiped itself clean. It had taken them ten years to discover that these virtues were called Alzheimer's. A few years after that, he was having to be fed like a fledgeling. Food had to be forced down his throat with a teaspoon so he wouldn't choke. But he was still greedy, keeping his mouth open for more, sometimes smacking his lips and letting out long, resonant burps. Granny cared for him with unsentimental vigour. When he had lost everything, he forgot to live and died in his wife's arms, gazing into her eyes.

'I don't think sexual idiocy is a sign of good health. I think it's a sign of death,' remarked Théo.

'Are you thinking about Grandfather?' asked Bénédicte.

'Yes,' said Théo. 'Maybe he was dead long before he died. He was dead, but his desire for sex and laughter and food remained alive. It's like the way hair and fingernails carry on growing after death. No one hates hair or fingernails. And no one should hate sex or laughter or food either. But they should be wary of them. People shouldn't be so pleased, or proud, of screwing or eating or laughing. They shouldn't confuse them with being alive.'

Granny's flat was on the first floor of a large stone and brick house. Beneath its windows ran a broad avenue, lined with trees which tempered the cold winter winds and the still heat of summer. She no longer walked down its polished staircase, or along the long corridor leading to the front door. She was afraid of having a fall or of simply getting tired. So she stayed in her flat and only agreed to go to her hairdresser or her bank if someone went with her. Sometimes their cousins took her. She didn't expect visitors, now her son had left to set up home in a place she'd never visit. She didn't like travelling. For that matter she still felt a stranger in the town to which she had moved in her youth and in which she had lived for sixty years.

She was born in the mountains, in the Vosges, at Val-d'Ajol. As a child she had gone to school on skis, a journey that took more than an hour. Her father, an engineer, hunted and caught crayfish. There were photos of him posing among fir trees, hand on hip, on the banks of a mountain stream. One could see the foam on the white water very clearly. He had a moustache and a little hat with feathers in it and he leaned nonchalantly on the barrel of his gun.

She often describes her childhood, knowing the memory of that time will disappear with her, and hoping that her grandchildren will postpone the moment of absolute oblivion. She hopes that an image of her childhood will outlive her a little, an image of the time when she was still whole, tugging at the great skirt of her heavy, cheerful mother in the friendly hubbub of the kitchen. That everything won't disappear at the same time, this everything now greater than herself, this everything which also includes her family.

'I read in the paper yesterday,' Théo said, one day, 'that Val-d'Ajol has the highest number of suicides of any village in France.'

'I never thought of it like that,' said Bénédicte.

Granny's elder brother had committed suicide and her

younger brother had spent forty years in a mental hospital. She remained as indomitable as ever.

Théo rang the bell. It took her a little while to open the window and throw down a thin piece of string with the front door key attached to it. Bénédicte grabbed the key and opened the door. When she let go of it, the key rose back up the front of the house in little jerky stages. After going down the tiled corridor with its bluish pattern, they climbed the stairs, holding the banister. She was waiting for them outside her door, made-up, smiling, a voluminous white silk blouse hanging on her.

'I lock both my doors,' she said as they went into her hall, 'and I keep the key in the tureen on the dresser, there.'

She lifted the lid and tossed the key in. It landed with a faint clink.

'You need to know these things in case anything should happen to me.'

She walked ahead of them into the dining room. Its large windows overlooked a beautiful garden. In spring the spreading trees drew across them like a curtain, so you could only glimpse the round pond and the pavilion in the park beyond.

Almost fifty years ago, in the early hours of the morning, all the men of the street had been rounded up and made to stand in the pavilion. Ten of them had been chosen, at random, and shot. Among them, an old man, bearded, wearing a nightshirt, and a sixteen-year-old boy. Bénédicte would have liked to have seen a photo of this youth, to have known what he looked like. She who, forty years after the execution, knew about his short life and his death, but did not know his name.

On the black linoleum further inside the flat, they used to take off their shoes and play oceans. The two of them would sit on a knitted blanket – the boat – and sail between continents, discover islands, sometimes anchor in the secret shadows under the desk. The crossings were dangerous and full of incident, because the Organisation de l'Armée Secrète blew up the safe-havens and bombarded ships. Another child was going to be born soon. But they didn't care; the most important thing was to master the ocean, the ocean and its wondrous perils.

In the early days of the war, the second world war, Granny remembers having to flee down the street during bombing raids. She remembers it very well and tells them about it. She saw a little girl crying and running through the crowd without her parents. She saw horses which had been blown to pieces by little steel balls, lying in the ditches. She saw a decapitated woman stretched out in the middle of her belongings, which had been torn apart and strewn along the edge of a field.

She was used to seeing people die, because she had been a nurse and had risen to become the principal of a nursing school. The thick textbooks arranged on the top shelf of her bookcase are her own work. She wrote and proofed them at night, while her grandchildren slept.

She can be seen in photos, smiling, strong and thickset. The white headscarf with a red cross tightly frames her round, monastic face. As a nurse she inflicted great painful remedies on her grandchildren when they were little. She administered massive injections, which she'd stick in their buttocks after taking down their underpants and laying them face-down on the kitchen table. She smeared their private parts with a brown lotion that burned.

She knows how people die and the different kinds of death caused by different illnesses. Face-twisting cholera, for instance, which drains the body and turns it black. Leprosy; the plague; tuberculosis which rips out the lungs. But the worst death, one she describes in a steady voice, is that caused by diphtheria, the croup which kills children. A white membrane gradually spins its web across the throat. The child can't drink or eat and eventually dies of suffocation. Then the family thinks it will die, in turn, of grief; flowers are brought for the little corpse. But who are the bouquets for? For the elder sisters who have just got engaged? Or for the little brother who has just expired? It's terrible how long it takes the membrane to suffocate the child. It's terrible to hear that slow death swelling and inexorably invading. Granny knows about another kind of death with which she often compares it: the death of a child who's swallowed caustic soda.

At night, Bénédicte struggled with this. She wondered if this death could be avoided. Perhaps she should be watching for the onset of croup. Her new siblings are so delicate. When death came too close and its hubbub grew too deafening, she would get up and put on her dressing gown and go and sit in the little ones' room. Beside their cot she would listen to their thin breathing. She'd watch for the moment they became agitated. Was there really no way of anticipating it – even in the safety of your own home? But Granny would shake her head with a little smile. There was no reply to the omnipotence of death.

'The bitch,' says Théo, 'she could have told you about vaccination.'

'She could have,' responds Bénédicte. 'But still, someone let the cat out of the bag in the end. And that day life

suddenly seemed incredibly benevolent. I felt like I had
snatched you away from certain death, and kept you safe
for years to come. I was as proud as if I'd invented vaccines
myself.'

'Too sensitive,' Granny used to say, 'these children are far
too sensitive.'

Among her books Granny had a square book illustrated
with black-and-white photos. Its title was *The Massacre at
Oradour-sur-Glane*. After Granny had told them the story of
how the village was attacked, the baker shut up in his oven,
the women and children crammed into the church and the
church set on fire, she would take the book down and give
them a commentary on the photos. In the last picture, it
was true, they could clearly see on the church walls the
marks left by the fingernails of the people who had been
burned alive.

Granny's survey of human death grew in both scale and
depth when she discussed the Nazi extermination camps.
She had all the newspaper reports. As a Catholic living in
the Vosges she had spent the war hunting for butter and
eggs. But she had lamented the disappearances, without
time for farewells, of her hairdresser and her Jewish stu-
dents. Sitting beside her on the blue sofa, Bénédicte had
listened quietly, clenching her hands and knees, desperately
trying not to ask any questions. She learned about death by
suffocation in the sealed lead wagons, about those who had
died from starvation walled up in windowless cells – sometimes singing – about those who had died of exhaustion and
dysentery, those who had been gassed and found crushed
together, those who had been accused of conspiracies and
hung from meat hooks. Granny would raise her head and

point to her jugular: *There*, she'd say, with a sweep of her crooked finger. The mothers and children, the ones who'd trampled each other, the ones who'd given themselves up, the ones who'd lost their minds before losing their lives. And lastly those who had come home too tormented to live, who had died before they could regain their lives.

By the time she'd concluded these stories Granny had achieved one of her probable aims. Bénédicte was no longer afraid of death. She saw it as the mark of divine compassion, the great solution to the otherwise infinite sufferings of mankind. From then on she found nothing more soothing than watching a proper shoot-out on the television on Sundays. She also became completely unable to give herself up to sleep. She dealt with her fear of the dark by lying awake, reading. By adolescence, when sleep returned to her, she possessed a vast store of miscellaneous knowledge, eroded by tiredness.

When Bénédicte had grown up a little and become a little less sensitive, took it all a little less to heart, the only deaths that Granny talked to her about were those of her relatives. That of Charles, not yet twenty, who had screamed for a whole night as he lay wounded in No-Man's-Land at Verdun, whom no one had been able to help, and who hadn't died until morning. That of Charles's mother, whose tears were all spent by the time someone came to tell her of her son's death, and whom Granny had watched over patiently. That of her own mother, whose slow, peaceful passing she had also accompanied for days and months. That of Uncle André, shipwrecked in his little sailboat, his leg broken by another boat which fled in the storm and left the fatally wounded man to drown. These spectacular deaths seemed a homely litany, a heroic and bloody family album. The children felt proud of their memories of the relatives they'd had time to know, who had in their turn enrolled them in the prospect of death.

Then Granny grew old. The woman who had spent her life treating other people's bodies now grew engrossed in the meaning of the soul.

Nursemaid and guardian of her husband's Alzheimer's, she read a great deal, prayed a great deal, and grew angry with God for not answering her. She didn't hesitate to challenge him in front of the grandchildren. Eventually she accepted it and came to a kind of understanding with Him such as would not insult her intelligence. As she continued to age, she approached her own death. And – as often happens – when she was close to that moment at last, she forgot all about it and instead followed the daily betrayals of her body with horror.

The three of them sat at the round table. Granny had drawn the blinds halfway in order to keep out the park sunshine. She had made tea, slowly, and taken some stewed fruit out of the refrigerator for Théo, who had a delicate digestion.

'I hope you're eating properly now.'

Neither Théo nor Bénédicte dared smoke, for fear of being told the true and exhaustive story of Uncle Georges's death from lung cancer – similar to croup but more painful and deserved.

While Théo ate his stewed fruit, Granny took them through the saga of her heart, her valves, her aortas and her arteries, her veins and her veinlets and all those fine old dysfunctions which now occupied her time. She took the instructions out of the boxes of medicine and read them aloud. She asked questions. 'You see this big vein which goes into the heart – here – can you remember what it's called?'

She was silent, then resumed, looking a little defeated, 'I feel old.' She told them about not being able to write any more, how tired reading made her, the incredible struggle her mind waged with her absconding memory. Théo sobbed discreetly into his fruit. Bénédicte, refusing to cry, was silently bored to tears.

Abruptly, Granny broke off and looked at them. They were pale, tired, dazed by the sun, two absurd and not particularly touching figures. She laughed a clear, cascading laugh. Her laughter seemed like a song, tumbling down a mountain. It splashed over them.

'I'm boring you,' she said. 'But,' she added piteously, 'I'm going to die soon and I'm afraid.'

'Yes,' said Théo.

'What do you expect us to say to that?' said Bénédicte.

'Nothing,' said Granny. 'Tell me about you.'

So they talked, in no particular order, assembling little anecdotes they'd chosen to amuse her. She listened to them with a kindly, mischievous smile, bending her head to hear better and asking little artless questions when they paused.

Bénédicte took the tea tray into the kitchen and stacked the cups in the sink. Granny followed her in and watched her.

'I haven't got any muscles any more,' she said suddenly. 'It's terrible, they've all gone. They just slip away, can you believe it?'

She unbuttoned the top of her blouse, revealing her shoulders and her thin arms.

'Poor Granny,' said Bénédicte. She looked away; she contemplated jumping out of the window.

'I shouldn't be showing you this,' remarked Granny. She buttoned up her blouse. When she looked back up at Bénédicte, her eyes were full of liquid, water, tears. She stayed there, upright, her arms dangling at her sides.

'It's hard being all on your own,' she said.

Bénédicte went towards her and took the body that had once been so strong in her arms. She clasped the old woman as though she were holding a child, imprinting her with all her strength. It seemed to her that some of her heat was transferred in the tight embrace. She bitterly regretted not being able to shelter her for longer, having to return her body to her. She wished she could take into herself, into her warm, firm womb, Granny's fragile, familiar, escaping life. It's cruel – not being able to restore life the way one can give it. She released Granny from her grip with the terrible feeling that she was abandoning her.

'Oh, damn,' she said.

She bent down to kiss Granny's neck and squeeze her thin shoulders between her palms. Then, hugging her again, she lifted Granny off the ground. Granny laughed, a little dishevelled, her blouse untucked from her skirt.

'Well,' she said, 'I shouldn't talk about myself so much.' With unconvincing submissiveness, she added, 'I should put my life in God's hands.'

'That's right,' said Bénédicte, 'and don't forget to ask for a receipt.'

The effort of paying them so much attention had worn Granny out. Her face had crumpled and her eyelids had begun to droop, her expression had grown increasingly vague. They left, waving out of the car windows, at once sorry and relieved. Granny waved farewell from the kitchen window. She looked like a princess locked in a tower by a

witch, condemned to watch the world through a na
arrow slit. They had left her exhausted by conversation
wanting to return to her anxious silence.

'So, what do we do now?' said Bénédicte. She was driving
again, and smoking, chewing on the filter of her cigarette.

'We could go to the park,' suggested Théo. 'Are you
hungry?'

In the middle of the park, near the pond, there was a
large café with a terrace. In summer, families and people at
a loose end sat there, keeping an eye on their children on
the swings, or watching their friends rowing on the pond.
Tram rails skirted the gardens nearby, hidden by a screen of
chestnut trees.

Bénédicte parked the Alfa in the shade of the tall trees.
Théo got out, sighing. They walked in single file down the
flower-bordered path that led to the pond. The shouts of
children hanging in clusters on the climbing frame rose like
smoke into the cloudless sky, bouncing off each other in
shrill plumes. The mothers, in light-coloured dresses, displayed their white legs to the sun. Sipping Martinis, they
spoke in hushed voices to their young lovers who wore
short-sleeved shirts and smoked mentholated cigarettes. At
intervals along the path tall, long-legged children perched
nervously on their bicycles.

Bénédicte and Théo sat down at an empty little round
table in the shade of an acacia and waited in silence for the
waiter to take their order. He returned with big, golden-
brown waffles, their crunchy squares hiding a sweet paste
which was still warm and runny.

'Have you got a phone card?' asked Théo as he cut up his
waffle.

'...no do you want to call?'

'...)oesn't matter.'

...He lifted his face up from his plate. The fine icing sugar ...d settled in a cloud round his lips.

'I feel a long way away from everything. I can't understand things. I'm like an English explorer who's reached the banks of a great African river. He goes to the villagers' market all alone, surrounded by colours and noise. He is very precisely at the end of the world. I'm like him: happy but lost. I think that this particular acute feeling of exile can drive you mad.'

'Don't go mad,' said Bénédicte. 'Make the phone call.'

'When I phone,' continued Théo, 'I stay in touch with the familiar world. People will know that I'm here. If I disappeared, my trail would be picked up. That reassures me.'

Bénédicte took a wad of stuck-together paper from the back pocket of her trousers. She broke it apart and extracted a phone card, which she laid on the table in front of them.

Théo swallowed a last piece of waffle, took the card and stood up. 'I'm going to look for a phone box,' he said.

Bénédicte stayed by herself, leaning on her elbows, watching the little groups gathered on the terrace.

She looked. She looked more and more deeply, feeling caressed by the sun that tumbled through the branches of the acacia. She felt drowsy. The world seemed round to her, perfectly round, a plastic bag inflated with ether, a mossy cave in the bulb of a mushroom. Leaning on her elbows, her cheek in her hands, she felt her sight sinking inside herself. She started blinking, casting a veil over the terrace and the pond and distancing the children's hubbub to a whisper.

The world curled over on itself like a warm ball. In the

middle of it she laid down as a garland the memory of the people she loved and those she had loved. She sank into the certainty of a dream, a delirium of harmony. The world is round, she thought, not a cube or a pyramid, but a sphere filled with a great espaliered tree. It is much less cruel and sharp than people think. Maybe it's enough to let oneself be carried along like a balloon, floating around the espalier. No one leaves this round world and all of us are included in it, the living and the dead, swimming like ethereal bubbles. Bénédicte's eyes had closed completely and she was just feeling her elbows giving way under the weight of her head when Théo suddenly grabbed the back of her chair.

She opened her eyes and, staring at him gravely, said, 'Stop smoking. I don't want you dying on me.'

'At least someone doesn't,' said Théo. He started crying, silently, his shoulders shaking.

'It's nervous exhaustion,' said Bénédicte, leaning on the parapet of the small bridge.

The rowers passed beneath them, striking the water with their oars. Théo sniffed and blew his nose on a big grey scrumpled handkerchief.

'I'm scared,' he said.

He continued to cry. Bénédicte drummed her fingers on the rail.

'It's because you're tired,' she said eventually in a peremptory tone. 'You're far too tired.' She looked at him authoritatively.

'Do you think so?' said Théo, sneaking a look at her. Gradually his sniffing came to a halt.

'Everybody has fragile moments,' she said, after a few seconds' thought. 'You remind me of women who have just brought a child into the world. They're tired, but more than that, they're empty. It's as if they've become porous and the whole world surges in through their pores. They cry when they see a little animal, when they see people in the street, when it's a beautiful day, when it's raining. They can't bear anything any more because they've undertaken to bear everything. They've got the space – the one they've made in themselves for the child – to take in every sensation. People call that depression. But that's stupid. It's just that it's unbearable to be so porous. Some people are like those women, always carrying within them things which fill them up and dispossess them. You're too porous.'

'But why is everything that happens to me so horrible?' said Théo.

'Because you're a nutter.'

She took him by the arm and they walked back through the park, along the twisting paths lined with green benches. She talked constantly, punctuating her speech with emphatic gestures. Now and again a word would catch on him, and she'd massage that word's essence until its capacity to inflict pain had dissolved. By the time they reached the car, they were laughing. She was in full flow, overwhelming him with her disorganized and contradictory assertions, and as brilliant and sparkling as a magic lantern, thanks to him.

'Let's get out of here,' said Théo, as soon as he was back in the passenger seat. 'Let's go home, there's nothing here any more.'

> *We'll step up and take the reins*
> *When our elders bid adieux*
> *And we'll hear their constant refrain*

And the echo of their virtues
And the e-e-echo of their virtues

With its windows wide open, the Alfa negotiated the bends recklessly, grinding against the kerb or swerving wildly into the middle of the road. They sang at the tops of their voices, Bénédicte, square-shouldered, guiding the steering wheel with her fingertips and Théo sitting cross-legged, beating time with his hand. He wore a large pair of sunglasses with pale horn-rimmed frames which Bénédicte had dug out of the bottom of her bag and given to him, saying, 'Here, you'll be able to see the road.'

Before she'd passed him the case, she'd taken out the glasses and examined them. 'I bought them four years ago for a holiday. Wait, they're designer, I think.' She checked the inside of one of the arms. 'Yes, it says *Christian Dior*.'

She put them on her nose. The frame threw her whole face out of kilter.

'I wanted to be, sort of . . . like a lady. I wanted to look like a lady.'

She turned to Théo. She looked like a fly, all eyes.

'Not very successful, eh? I don't know why these disguises never work with me. Any old bimbo can carry them off. Even guys can learn how to do it. Transvestites. They know things that I don't. Or do you think it's a question of bone structure?'

Théo, who was looking ahead and listening to his sister with one ear, distractedly picked his nose.

'No, it's a question of sunglasses,' he said. 'Not bone structure, sunglasses. Your life will be a lot simpler when you've understood that. Give them to me.'

He perched the pale horn-rimmed frames on his nose. He looked like a sunglasses thief.

And we'll hear their constant refrain
And the echo of their virtues

They joined the motorway just before Lille. The asphalt ribbon gleamed, shaping mirages in the fading light.

'Put your seat belt on,' said Bénédicte.

'Maybe,' said Théo. He put his seat belt on. 'Can you get your head round the fact that one day Granny is going to die?'

'Yes, I can. Look: One day, Granny is going to die. It's taken me quite a while, but I've done it.'

'Well,' said Théo, pushing the glasses up to the bridge of his nose, right against his eyebrows, 'can you get your head round the fact that one day one of us is going to die?'

The Alfa swerved sharply. The motorway was filled with the strident blaring of lorries' horns. Flashing headlights lit up the inside of the car.

'Shut up, fat-arse juggernaut,' Bénédicte said into the rearview mirror. She turned towards Théo.

'You're a bastard,' she said.

'I'm a bastard,' he agreed. 'But at least I'm a porous bastard. And keep your eyes on the road or we'll end up in a ditch.'

He put on a tape. His eyelids slowly closed and his head lolled against the window. He was asleep. Bénédicte took one hand off the steering wheel and shifted her weight on to her hip to get at the lighter in her pocket. She lit a cigarette. They'd be in Paris at about nine.

An extract from *Sans Moi* by Marie Desplechin,
also available from Granta Books

1

'Thanks, I'd love some more,' said Olivia, taking the handle
of the saucepan. 'I've got a confession to make. God, I
should stop eating so much, I'm blowing up like a balloon . . . Do you remember when I first came here, in
September?'

'Yes,' I said. 'It's still only October, after all.'

'Oh. Right. Well, I've got to tell you this. I hadn't
stopped taking drugs back then. I admit it.'

'Uh huh.' I reached for my cigarettes.

'But I have now.'

I lit a cigarette unhurriedly, blew a smoke ring, and said,
'I knew.'

'You knew what?'

'I knew you were taking drugs.'

Olivia wiped her plate with a piece of bread in silence.
She didn't look up. Maybe she didn't believe me, or perhaps
she was hurt.

'You could have just kicked me out. People don't like
babysitters using drugs.'

'If it'd been anyone else, I would have.' I didn't say anything else.

She got up from the table and cleared away our plates,
piling them noisily on top of each other.

'Do you want some coffee?' she asked, going into the
kitchen.

could hear her in there, muttering about the little presso maker. I'd screwed the top on too tightly and she couldn't open it.

'The fact is,' I shouted, 'I didn't sack you because I trust you . . . Can you hear me? Because I'm fond of you.'

A furious groan came from the kitchen, followed by a familiar crash.

'Don't worry,' Olivia called out. 'It's not serious, it's only the glasses.'

As a rule, we appreciate the love of our fellow human beings either as a necessary acknowledgement of our worth or as a surprise that seems heaven sent. We have been raised for it, one way or another – by being starved or over-indulged, it doesn't really matter. When it comes down to it, we love to be loved and we love to love, maybe misguidedly and to our cost, but deliberately, stubbornly and repetitively. Love pleases us, with its rattle of chains and periodic windfalls. Good thing too. There's nothing more desolate than hating love.

Olivia was caving in under the weight of her problems. Having experienced neither starvation nor over-indulgence, only absence and chaos, she was as mistrustful of other people's feelings as a petty criminal.

'Did someone say something to you?' she asked, slapping two sugars down on the table next to my cup.

'No,' I said. 'I guessed. It wasn't that hard.'

In order to confirm my suspicions, one morning I'd summoned to my flat my brother Laurent, a family counsellor, and his friend Thierry, an expert in the field, partly reformed but full of regrets and prone to relapses.

'Tell him what you told me on the phone,' my brother

said, sitting on the old Fender amplifier which presided over the trestle table in my flat.

I poured a cup of coffee.

'OK. Well, some evenings she doesn't say a word and she's really down, and then the next day she's all excited and bright-eyed and can't stop talking.'

'Yes,' said the expert.

'She talks the whole time about the pills she's taking or that she used to take and about drinking, but she swears: drugs, no way, what a bloody liability, when you see how it messes people up, especially girls, all the things you can't do when you're into it and how they all end up, no teeth and on the game, and so on and so forth. Unless you're in it up to your eyeballs, I don't see how anybody could go on about it so much.'

'Sure,' the expert said, looking concerned. He wasn't much of a talker.

'Guys are always ringing up and she doesn't want to talk to them, it's as if she's scared. Then there's Captain Hook and Long John Silver, in and out of her room at all hours of the day and night, carrying bags and acting like big shots – the concierge is going crazy with suspicion. Then there's the packages she has to deliver, by taxi – who to and with what money, I've no idea. One evening she told me that she'd taken my daughter with her to drop something off. A trip in a taxi, that's fun for a kid. I said no, there's nothing fun about it and that from now on there is going to be no more talk of packages or taxis.'

'Well done. Any other signs?'

'The tin foil keeps going missing from the kitchen.'

'Oh no!' said the expert. 'Tin foil's a problem. A big problem.'

He hunched over his coffee.

'You see?' said Laurent.

'No chance this'll sort itself out,' the expert diagnosed, scratching his sparse hair in dismay. 'Every chance it'll get worse.'

'You're fucked,' concluded Laurent. 'She's got to go. We can tell her, if you like.'

'No,' I said, 'let me sort this out. It's a special case.'

At that point, my brother left for work and the dismayed expert stayed behind with me. We went to bed straight away since it was only casual between us – to my great displeasure. I would have preferred a little regularity.

'The hardest thing,' I told Olivia, so she'd understand all the anxiety she'd caused me, 'was that I didn't want you to leave.'

'Because of the children?'

'Yes. But because of me as well. I didn't want to sack you, I didn't want to give you a hard time. I just wanted you to stop taking drugs.'

Of the prize-winning line-up of liars and addicts life had thrown up for me to become attached to, it was clear that she took the palm, the laurel wreath, the roar of the crowd and the entire triumphal arch. It was also clear, from the day we met, that I felt as if I'd known her for ever. Don't get me wrong. I'm not saying I felt I knew what kind of life she'd had but she struck me as someone I'd always known – the features of her face, the way she laughed and suddenly turned sad. I could tell her socks in the washing machine by their colours. I could recognize her creases in the ironing.

Let's say we'd experienced the same fears and hardships and had the same kind of childhood. Or let's say that we were the same age. Smoked the same cigarettes. Wore the same nail varnish. But none of this was the case. I was ten years older than her and our lives were as foreign to one another as a Joanna Trollope novel is to a Hubert Selby short story.

'What about your friends, Agnès and all that lot who sent me to you? Did you ask them?'

'Of course. They all swore no, no drugs, ever. They thought it was amazing, really, considering what you'd been through: no drugs and no prostitution – for a girl who's been in care and lived on the street and seen what she's seen, it's practically a miracle; you can take her on with complete confidence. What's more, she loves children.'

Olivia giggled. She adored people she could make fools of.

'You can't hold it against them. They didn't know. Jean-Luc, Dominique and Agnès, they're innocent. I wouldn't ever have wanted them to suspect.'

'You remind me of a girl I used to know ten years ago. A girl from Savoy. She had tiny blue eyes, thin lips and shoulders like a wrestler. I got her a job at my work. "I wouldn't say I've never touched drugs," she used to say to me, "but all that's over now, it was too much." At lunch she'd tell me about all the tragic things she'd been through, her father who worked in a slate quarry, her twelve brothers and sisters and what a cruel place the world was. The next morning she'd come to the office still a complete mess from the night before, with her clothes all crumpled and white specks round her nostrils and fall asleep on the switchboard. She went mad when someone suggested she should clean up and go into detox and then one morning she left with the four thousand francs I'd lent her; I was earning seven at the time. It made me sad that she could just disappear like that, even though we were friends. I've never seen her again. Maybe she's dead.'

'Maybe,' said Olivia. 'Addicts always end up being bastards, that's just the way they are.'